the Clean

THE CLEAN © 2026 by Hope Swan
The rights of Hope Swan, as the author of the Work, has been asserted.
All rights reserved.

First published by Wattle Tree Press, Australia, 2026.
www.wattletreepress.com

Apart from use permitted and sanctioned by the author, this publication may not be reproduced, stored, or transmitted, in any form, or by any means, without express permission from the author. Quotes may be used for the purpose of reader reviews. Any use of this publication to "train" or otherwise engage with any form of generative artificial intelligence, in any capacity, regardless of how the publication was obtained or procured, is expressly prohibited, unless licensed by the author. For permissions and licensing, contact the author at www.hopeswan.com.au

This is a work of fiction. The story described herein is not a statement of fact and should not be taken as such. The characters, settings, dialogue and incidents are products of the author's imagination and should not be construed as real. Any resemblance to persons living or dead is coincidental. The opinions expressed are those of the characters and should not be confused with the author's.

A catalogue record for this book is available from the National Library of Australia

The Clean
Cover: Wattle Tree Press
Interior: Wattle Tree Press
Editor: Tara Jean
ISBN: 978-1-7640785-2-8 (print)
ISBN: 978-1-7640785-1-1 (ebook), 978-1-923423-16-9 (Kindle ebook)

Never let anyone tell you that you are less than them because of an illness or disability.

You are more than worthy of anything they are.

THE CLEAN TRILOGY: BOOK 1

HOPE SWAN

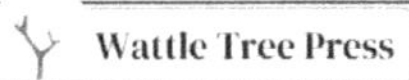

1

Prologue

Designations: an inexplicable etching on the skin, similar to a tattoo, which can appear as soon as something happens to the body. There have been studies, but no one knows why they occur, or why they only show up in certain individuals.

My first designation showed up three days after my birth.

As I eventually got told, my mother screamed as the cursive word etched itself across my tiny stomach.

UPSET.

That's right. I got my first designation because baby Scarlett had an upset stomach. Or perhaps it was because I was only three days old and babies are frequently upset, correct? Definitely my fault …

The second one came when I was three months old – my mother

accidentally knocked my knee on a cabinet.

INTERNAL BLEEDING.

Designations are awfully dramatic, don't you think? I got only a bruise.

I was four years old, with a few designations, when the government declared the "Written" were dangerous – a risk to the "Clean's" health. Then, they gave the Written "perks" like a curfew and limited access to the city of Lait at large. Written could only live and work in the Third Quarter, with a very occasional exception given to the best doctors and scientists.

It's funny, Lait's government had never had an issue with us until that point, and no one knows why their opinions changed so drastically. People have their theories, many surrounding our king, who married into Lait royalty, but nobody really knows.

Prior to the Written reforms, we were side-eyed, looked down on if our families couldn't afford erasure machines, but for the most part, we were still accepted in society. As the divide between the Clean and the Written grew, children began to be dumped at the Third Quarter boundary and left to fend for themselves.

Now, the Written population are increasingly uneducated and considered nothing more than wasted space. It's been years since any have been allowed to formally study.

So, can you see why I was sceptical when the government

announced a university program for the most intelligent Written? At the most prestigious school in Lait, no less? It's not like we had a baseline education; the Written with high IQs are simply naturally intelligent. Some of us may have had books growing up, but that's where it ends.

Why the hell would the Clean want to give us any kind of leg up in the world?

That's just it ... They don't.

2

Scarlett

It's beyond unusual to see a group of people huddled around the notice boards by the market, and even more surprising that others keep joining them. Cursing myself and my curiosity, I nudge my way in behind them, craning my neck to get a look at whatever has interested so many.

The usual notices – livestock sales and the occasional announcement – are covered by one large poster.

ON BEHALF OF THE LAIT ROYAL FAMILY AND GOVERNING BODIES:

Resisting the urge to scoff, I shove my way closer to get a better look.

We are honoured to announce a new initiative bridging the

gap between the Clean Lait community and the Written Lait community.

Twenty-five Written community members will receive a full scholarship to the Royal Bennett University.

Please keep an eye on these boards tomorrow for the announcement of this lucky group. These citizens will leave the Third Quarter by 8:00am on the 31st.

Three days.

The government is letting out a group of Written in three days. This is unheard of.

The word "will" insinuates this isn't an invitation but a demand.

The group that has gathered is swapping theories back and forth.

Is this a trick?

Will these poor people be used as examples? Flogged in the market for having hope?

Or maybe, just maybe, this could be legitimate …

But for what reason? My mind runs through dozens of theories.

Turning away from the crowd, I make the quick walk back to my share house in record time. I'm greeted by a chorus of voices as I throw open the door into the kitchen, revealing three of my roommates sitting around the communal, ancient and almost falling apart, kitchen table.

Zaid, Riley and Tilly eye me curiously, whatever they were talking about, forgotten.

My fourth roommate, Levi, has his back to me, scavenging through our fridge for what I can only assume is his lunch. I attempt to ignore the uptick in my heart rate and look anywhere except at the muscles I see flexing through his shirt – I'm just a girl, after all.

"Scar!" Tilly starts, breaking the others from their daze.

"Scar Scar!" Zaid smirks, and I stick my tongue out. Zaid is a great friend, but he's gotten more annoying after his boyfriend, Asher, moved in with my friend Mia. She gleefully told Zaid stories from when we were younger, which he now teases me with relentlessly.

"Scaranator!" Riley laughs, another nickname that Mia was all too happy to fill them in on.

I'm considering heading down the road to her house to curse her out when Levi breaks me from my thoughts.

"Hey Scarlett," Levi says, his smooth voice giving me butterflies. With my eyes still roaming over his back, and mind thinking things it shouldn't about my best friend, I grin.

"Levi." I nod, moving past the table as I push my backpack off my shoulder and give it no further thought when it lands by the leg in a crumpled heap.

"Did you see it, Scar?" Tilly asks, an odd look sweeping over her face.

Tills is like the younger sister none of us got to have. She'd been alone for a long time by the time Levi found her at the market four years ago, only days away from complete starvation. Nobody had ever seen someone with so many designations, her fair skin almost entirely covered. She was terrified when Levi brought her back to the house, only opening up after weeks of reassurance and careful approaches.

As a Written born to Clean parents, they had abandoned her in the Third Quarter when she was very young. Tilly wasn't sure how old she was because her parents had never kept count. She estimated about eight. The sheer amount of time she had spent fighting out in the world on her own meant that she had become malnourished and underdeveloped. Most Written can barely afford to look after themselves, so she had been ignored.

It's not that the other Written don't want to help the homeless, because most of us do, but when you struggle to survive yourself, your ability and desire to help others lessens.

During Tilly's first year of living with us, I caught myself venting to Levi multiple times. Tilly was so kind-hearted, sweet and resilient, and her parents had just left her. Anger would course through my veins every time I thought about it. For reasons unknown to me, Tilly claimed she loved her mother, but why? It vexed me to no end. Tilly said little about her past, except that it was her father that left her; she's always been adamant about that.

Eventually, Levi had to sit me down, insisting that we were her family now and there was no point in focusing on the past.

After everything she's been through, I could never lie to her.

"Yeah, I did Tills."

Jumping up and down excitedly, she grabs my arm. "I'm sure it's going to be you! It has to be!"

My stomach churns at the possibility, but I try my hardest to smile. Tilly means well, but she doesn't understand what being chosen would entail. Hell, I don't understand it. "There are so many special people here Tills, it could be anyone."

With her hands still clasped tightly to my arm, she shakes her head. "There's no one like you."

To be quite honest, I don't do well with emotion. I never have. You can't afford to feel in the Third Quarter as a Written.

"Thanks, Tills." I shake her hands off, moving over to the fridge, praying that Riley has cooked something on his day off from the market, where he single-handedly runs everyone's favourite food stall, a kitchen he refuses to give a name to because he frames himself as a "chef to all people."

I thank every god I know the name of when I find the fridge full. Grabbing as much as I can hold in one go, I close the door with my foot, only to be greeted by Levi's raised eyebrow.

"What?" I sarcastically throw in his direction, daring him to say something stupid.

Stifling back a laugh, Levi walks towards me as the others dart out, Zaid muttering something about an early start the next day. "Hungry?"

"No shit."

Corralling me over to the table, he sits down on the chair opposite. "You realise she could be right?"

"Who? Tilly?"

Levi nods, shooting me a look I know too well – his "I know something that you don't" look – "I heard Marcia talking about it at the clinic today. She thinks they're looking for intelligence."

"When have you ever believed a word Marcia says? She's a gossip."

"The mayor, Scarlett. Marcia heard it straight from the mayor's mouth."

Now that ... that made me freeze, Riley's chicken pie forgotten. The Third Quarter is the only Lait quarter with a mayor, because the Royals fear us too much to govern us themselves. However, that also means our mayor is the only person in direct contact with the palace.

"How do we know she's telling the truth?"

Levi sighs, "You know she wouldn't lie about that. Marcia may like drama, but she doesn't fuck around with official stuff."

Looking down at my food, my heart thumps a million times over in my chest. I sit in silence, considering that Tilly may be right … this could happen to me. I could get chosen.

Levi stands up, placing a large hand on my shoulder. I would never tell him, but his hand is warm, comforting, and I know I shouldn't think about how nice his touch is, but I'm only human.

"I've seen your file. An IQ of one hundred and thirty-two? If smarts are what they're looking for, Scarlett? They'll be coming for you."

As much as I don't want to admit it, he's right. Intelligence isn't really something that matters in the Third Quarter, but it *is* something that gets recorded – along with every other "vital" statistic of each Written person. We are at the bottom of Lait's society, but we are also its most watched.

Scoffing, and also hoping to deflect the attention, I stand up, my chair making a horrible grating sound that echoes around our tiny kitchen. "What about you? One hundred and twenty isn't exactly *dumb*, Levi."

We never went out of our way to read each other's files, but after Levi started at the small medical clinic, we had one night where we drank a little too much and ended up using his spare key to read through our files. Our little friend group was one of the few that had been old enough at the time of getting dropped off at the quarter to be able to read.

Our night turned into a semi-morbid, semi-amusing drinking game – who had the most designations? Drink! Who had the highest IQ? Drink!

We're smart, not immune to the effects of alcohol.

Levi shakes his head. "They're not going to take me away from the clinic. Every Written they can get working in there means one less Clean they have to send into the quarter."

Scarlett Weatherwood

Levi Smith

… … …

The list. It's here. Our names … right at the top.

Standing at the notice board reading our names is the most terrifying and exciting thing that has ever happened. Scanning the rest of the sheet, I regard the other names. There's only one other

I recognise – Thaddeus Michael – all the rest show information stating they are all different ages and from different sides of the quarter. I don't want to be happy about it, but I kind of am. Maybe this is my chance to make a change.

Looking back over my shoulder at Levi, who stands with his body clenched, hands tight at his side, I smile meekly. "Told you."

With nostrils flared, Levi rolls his eyes at me and stalks off. Levi is a hothead. Always has been. I know he'll come around ... eventually. He's a passionate man who has only ever wanted the best for the Written, and I'm sure he'll wrap his head around this new arrangement soon enough.

Well, at least he better ... he only has two days.

The truck arrives on the thirty-first around six in the morning. Too early for my liking, but I was so nervous about what today would bring I hadn't slept well anyway.

Unlike the trucks that normally roll around the Third Quarter – which aren't that many; it's not like we can afford auto repairs – this one was silent ... almost too silent to be real. With large, polished white panels and huge tyres, this truck screams business. Levi grips my hand as the truck lurches to a stop in front of our house. Two guards swiftly jump down into the dirt.

One of them reaches into their breast pocket to pull out a tablet. With a quick swipe, he looks up at us both, his eyes a shocking blue. "Scarlett Weatherwood and Levi Smith?"

Letting my hand fall out of his grip, Levi nods and takes a confident step forward, his hand outstretched. I know he's anything but confident, but we agreed that we'd put up a united front. The Clean already think we're animals, and we refuse to give them any other reason to think so.

The guard takes one look at his hand and snorts.

"I'm not here for pleasantries, Smith."

Before Levi can reply, I step forward. "You're taking us from our homes. The least you could do is pay us some respect."

The other guard, who has been quiet until now, steps between us. He towers above me, and with the added black hair and dark eyes, he's a striking figure. "Written will follow orders that are given by the King or be tried as traitors. We are your superiors. If he says to kiss the dirt at his feet, you do so, without another word. Do you understand?"

My heart pounds a million miles an hour as he grabs my chin, bringing our eyes to meet. "Weatherwood, I assume?" Slowly, self-preservation kicks in and I nod. "You're lucky to be in this position. Don't forget that," he snaps. He removes his hand and pushes me away.

The guards motion for us to move around the back of the van. Both of them throw the doors open. The inside is nowhere near as nice as the exterior. Two metal benches sit across from each other, both already full of the other chosen Written. With a quick scan around, I work out that Levi and I are numbers twenty-three and twenty-four – with only one Written left to pick up before we head to the gate and leave the Third Quarter behind.

As we near the edge of the quarter, my confusion increases. They had specifically said twenty-five Written, and the list had confirmed that, so where was number twenty-five?

When my unquenchable curiosity can't take it anymore, I stand up and knock on the wall of the van, where I assume the two guards sit on the other side. Some of the other Written stare at me, worry etched into their tired-looking faces.

"Hey? Wasn't there meant to be twenty-five of us?"

"There was."

That asshole with black hair. It has to be. The response is too dry, too outwardly cruel. Plus, his voice is lower.

"There's only twenty-four people back here."

It's the other guard that responds this time, voice still cold and removed but with a kinder inflection. "Number twenty-five decided not to be present at pick-up."

"What do you mean?"

Getting no response, I bang on the wall again. "Hey! What happened to twenty-five?"

"Twenty-five is dead."

The first day at the university is the absolute definition of a whirlwind. Rules and regulations are pretty much spat at us, and each Clean we encounter is even less welcoming than the guards. We aren't permitted to stay at the university and are only allowed on campus four days a week, and we are never to directly interact with the Clean students unless given strict permission.

Prisoners outside of our prison.

Clearly, whoever made the call on this new program had not discussed this or collaborated with the students or professors.

It doesn't take long for our intelligence theory to be confirmed though, with the Dean implying that we are the "best" of the bad bunch.

It's the second day at university when everything really goes to hell.

Protests happen all over campus, where every Clean student is up in arms about having us around. The violence is maddening, and five Written students are killed. It isn't long before the university transforms the oldest and most run-down parts of the campus – previously abandoned – into special "Written Only" areas.

I find it unusual that they don't cancel this whole thing and instead choose to provide the Written with isolated classes. No Clean contact whatsoever aside from the teaching staff.

There's no doubt about it...

We are well and truly in enemy territory.

3

Matthew

As soon as I turned twenty-five, my father decided that the best way to prepare me for one day taking over as the head of Lait's military was to babysit my best friend. Or, as he called it, "Get put in charge of the Prince's personal security detail."

You know? Same shit, different smell.

Growing up under the guise of Lait's military controller was never easy. From day one, my father was overly vigilant and dead set on me following in his footsteps. If he had had his way, I would have been training with the other soldiers from the moment I could walk. My mother was the one who didn't let him, ensuring that he waited until the ripe age of ten to forcibly conscript me – yes ... that was sarcasm.

Tina South was my father's heart and soul, and she could convince him of anything except not to force me into combat. That decision was made and out of her control the moment they found out their second child would be a boy.

Henry Martins was a family man in public, and nowhere else.

Growing up with Flynn had been nice – neither of us could stray far from the castle, and after his mother nearly died in childbirth, the King and Queen decided that one heir was enough. My sister, who had been born when my parents were barely eighteen, never hung around for our "escapades" – we were just two young, annoying boys and she wanted nothing to do with us. She well and truly aspired to be the "big" sister, tagging along with my mother as soon as she realised that's where the adult women were.

Balancing my new duties of looking after Flynn and still trying to be his friend became my daily juggle. I wasn't used to telling him no ... and he wasn't used to hearing it.

It was about a month into my new role when I realised how important it was that I find a way to separate my friend from the Prince.

Flynn had been stressing out ever since his father had declared that a select few of the Written would be let into the First Quarter to attend the university. I never understood why it bothered him so much. He wasn't allowed to attend in person, only just having completed his undergraduate degree from the professors his father paid to travel to the castle. I can't imagine my father ever going to such lengths for me.

Flynn's anxiety regarding the Written had been sky high for years, ever since his father had announced the "Written" problem in Lait.

So, ignoring a couple of security protocols, I accompanied Flynn outside of the castle, with the hope of easing some of his anxiety, or at least forgetting about it for a bit. We headed down into the "Party District" and we were a couple of drinks in when a stunning girl with cascading red hair began to grind up against Flynn.

"Sorry, Miss, I'm going to need you to back up."

With a smoothness only Flynn could possess, he grabbed her by the hips, moving her closer. Over her shoulder, he shot me a pleading look.

I wish I could blame being drunk, but I was sober enough to know better when I rolled my eyes and let it go on. Only minutes later, my father would have had my head if he had seen me slip the bartender five hundred dollars to look the other way when Flynn grabbed her hand and pulled her into a back room.

I finished my drink and looked down at my watch and soon realised Flynn had been in the room for over half an hour. Steeling myself to see him in a position I never wanted to see, I stood up, wiping my hands on my pants and delaying for as long as possible before walking over to the door.

"Flynn?" I knocked.

No answer.

I knocked harder. "Mate, we gotta get back before your dad realises."

Still no answer.

Standing back from the door, I prepared to kick it in.

"One last chance!"

Silence.

Mustering strength from my years of training, I forced my foot through the door, sending it swinging off its hinges.

"Fuck!"

I couldn't believe it as I took in the scene; Flynn pressed against the wall, shirtless, the redhead, also shirtless, holding a knife to his neck.

"Don't move!" she yelled, her eyes darting back and forth between us.

Slowly, I brought my hands up, away from the gun and knife that were attached to my belt. "It's okay, Flynn." I nodded as his eyes met mine, wider and more frightened than I'd ever seen.

"Hi," I acknowledged the girl. "My name is Matthew Martins. My job is to keep his ass safe."

The girl scoffed, hold tightening on the knife she clasped. "I know who he is."

I walked towards her. "Can we talk? Please? Trust me, I'm the first person who wants to slit his throat. Can I ask why you are trying to?"

"He ruined my life."

Lifting an eyebrow, I met Flynn's eye. He was just as confused as I was. The girl started to cry, her hold on the knife loosening.

It was only once she brought her hands down that I saw the designations on her back, not quite covered by the intricate lace pattern of her bra. Without further thought, my training kicked in.

My knife lodged between her shoulder blades so quickly, she had no time to scream.

I killed two more people in the same month.

Flynn couldn't understand why I started to keep my distance emotionally, but every time I had to explain to my father why I had allowed the Prince to be in danger drove me further and further away. I love Flynn like my brother, but I couldn't keep treating him like a friend when he is my sole responsibility.

So, for my sake, and his, we moved away from being best friends, settling into a weird in-between that neither of us truly acknowledged.

4

Scarlett

After a full year on campus at Royal Bennet University, you'd think I'd be used to the attitudes and looks of the Clean students as they walk past – judging, snickering ... disgust. Normally, it's not so bad when I'm head down in the lab, but if Grenkwist looks at me sideways one more time, I swear I'm going to launch myself over this bench and give him his very own designation.

Yes, it's unusual for a Written to gain three designations in one day ... but I've had a rough one, okay?

This morning I tripped on my way to campus, my head absolutely throbbing from a migraine that just won't quit. And to top it off, a little scratch I'd gotten over the weekend has added some obvious designations to my body. Lab work is hard enough without my supervisor looking at me like I have three heads.

Briefly, I consider shooting him an unhinged grin to get him to retreat to his office like I normally would, but I think better of it; this week the Crown Prince is touring the campus, and I don't want to get questioned about why I'm in a lab without a supervisor.

"Miss Weatherwood, could you please complete the saline solution to add to the main pot?"

Instead of declaring that a five-year-old could make it and not someone with an IQ of one hundred and thirty-two, I get to work. It isn't worth the reprimand. As I add the last ingredient, the little bell above the lab door chimes.

Without looking backwards towards the door, I count three, no four, sets of feet. My ears prick up as Grenkwist rushes over, murmuring under his breath about how much of an "honour it is" and how he is "sorry about the presence of a Written" in the lab at the same time as the Prince. Like it isn't obvious that they'd taken the Prince to the most worn-down part of campus, where they "keep" us.

Scoffing under my breath, I begin to turn, the tray balanced in my shaking hands. Making sure to keep my view trained at my feet like a "good little Written," I begin the small walk back to my bench. Except despite my best efforts, I forget about the solution Grenkwist spilled earlier.

Cursing every god under the sun as I fall backwards – my stupid university-mandated lab slippers not helping me regain my footing at all – my back hits the hard, concrete floor … and it hurts.

Like, really bad.

"Fuck!"

"Miss Weatherwood!"

Double fuck.

Giving up all pretence of trying to be the perfect Written, I meet Grenkwist's gaze, where the asshole has the audacity to look mad beyond words. He's the one who caused this!

Without thinking, I retort to his stupid face, "What? You should have cleaned this up half an hour ago!"

I blindly swipe away someone's hand, not even bothering to look at who has tried to help. Clambering to my feet, embarrassment floods my veins – I don't need any fake sympathy. I'm surprised one of them even tried to touch a "dirty" Written.

"That'll be overtime. Cleaning the lab equipment. Two weeks," Grenkwist seethes in my direction and, without further ado, turns back to the group, who I am only now just getting a good look at.

Prince Flynn, a guard, another man in a different uniform, who must be of a higher military ranking, and the University Dean.

It's sort of surreal seeing the Prince in person after watching him on television and official announcements. He really does look like the Queen, with a stunning beauty.

"I'm sorry about her, Your Highness. She has quite a mouth on her. I've had her under my tutelage for a little under a month, and I'm sure it won't be long before she's listening properly." Resisting the urge to scoff, I school my face, not missing the underlying threat in Grenkwist's voice. The man is a wanker, plain and simple. But a wanker who has control and power over me, nonetheless. So, I need to behave.

Prince Flynn looks uninterested, standing behind the higher-ranking military man and the Dean, his face buried in a book. "Whatever," he murmurs, flicking to the next page.

The Dean coughs and steps forward, placing a hand on Grenkwist's infuriatingly white lab coat. He never does any actual work ... Grenkwist is a lot of things, but a proper scientist is not one of them.

"It's okay, Howard. We have full faith in you," the Dean says, turning to the man next to him who actually appears to be listening. "Professor Grenkwist is one of our best in the Written program. Miss Weatherwood is very lucky to be working with him."

I try not to laugh.

Really hard.

But the military man must hear something slip out.

His head shoots up, piercing blue eyes meeting my murky hazel ones. *Fuck, the military man is pretty.*

"You'd do better to teach her quicker, sir."

He is also an asshole. I am so over men thinking they have the right to treat me like shit – both Written and Clean alike.

The Dean ignores the remark and gestures back to the door. "Shall we continue on?" Military man nods and shoots the other guard a look, who places a hand on the Prince's back, ushering him from the room.

I smile meekly as Grenkwist turns his attention back to me, my hands clasped behind my back.

"Sorry?"

5

Matthew

I haven't forgotten that Flynn had his nose stuck in that book for the entire lab visit, and I am ready to yell at him as soon as we are in the privacy of his quarters that have been specially prepared on the campus for his week-long visit. It's more of a resort in here than a dorm. As soon as I shut the door and the Dean's footsteps fade from the hall, I wrench the book from Flynn's hands.

"Hey!" he yells as it topples to the ground, pages splaying on the floor.

Reaching out with my foot, I kick it away. "No. More."

Holding a hand to his chest, I watch my best friend go red in the face, a familiar sign of his anger. Something that has been happening a lot more since I became "guard" Matthew, not "friend" Matthew.

"What the fuck, Matt?"

"I should be asking you! You're the one who spent the entire morning reading!"

Flynn takes another step back, the anger draining from his face. "You're right. I'm sorry."

"Cry me a river, I know you don't enjoy being around the Written, but you're going to have to get used to it if you're to convince your father you want to stay here!"

Flynn has been falling further and further into bad habits for months; drinking, partying, sex. Of course, I get it. He's under a lot of pressure as the only heir to Lait's throne, but I started to really worry about him when he came close to an overdose. So, when he declared he wanted to do more study, even in his drug-fuelled daze, I clung onto that and begged the King to see that it would be good for him.

I worked my ass off to convince the King that he would be okay. Safe. Eventually the King agreed, but only if a guard went with him.

Guess who? And Flynn isn't exactly being considerate of what I want ... not that it matters in the slightest. Since he's the future king and I'm just his supposed best friend.

"I know," Flynn says quietly. As much as I want to step across the room and strangle him, I understand. Flynn's life has been very removed from the Written, and he has only ever had to be around a handful, and they were always under tight surveillance.

The redhead incident at the bar remains unmentioned. Its lasting effect on Flynn, however, is undeniable.

I remember the day King Xavier declared the Written to be dangerous like it was yesterday, despite only being seven-years-old. It was during our era of sneaking into the kitchens to scavenge whatever treats we could. We were cute, and we used it to our advantage.

Flynn's favourite token food prize was a cupcake covered in peppermint lollies – I know, I don't see why either – and with the reception for a visiting dignitary due that night, we knew the kitchen staff would be in full swing, baking up treats of all different kinds.

You know when little kids think they're being quiet, but actually aren't? Yeah, that was me and Flynn as we made our way through the less populated hallways, giggling and pushing each other along.

"Matthew."

My sister stopped us both in our tracks, the kitchen light so close yet crushingly out of reach as she addressed us. In our childish minds, it was like she'd appeared out of nowhere.

At sixteen-years-old, Arla was beautiful, and desperate to grow up. So much so that the dignitary visiting that night sought a political alliance with Lait by marrying their son to Arla when she turned twenty-one. This unnamed son was quite a bit older than her, and I didn't fully comprehend the oddness of the situation until I was older. The whole relationship thing, let alone marriage, was incomprehensible to my seven-year-old self.

"Hi Arla," I chimed cheerily. She stared down at us both, and I couldn't help but compare her to the photos I'd seen of mother at her age. They were so similar – blonde and graceful – beautiful.

"Don't 'hi' Arla me," she scolded.

"Hi Arla. You look pretty." Flynn giggled.

With a soft smile, my sister's gaze left me and turned to Flynn, who had stepped out from behind me and stood to my left. "Your Highness."

Rolling my eyes, I sighed as my sister looked at him fondly. Flynn had developed his crush on Arla that year and had tried, to no avail of course, to convince the King to ask my father to give Arla's hand in marriage to him when he became of age.

"You shouldn't be down here. There are already foreign dignitaries walking around the palace."

Puffing out my chest, I tried my hardest to act like I'd seen my father do so many times. "I thought they were our allies?"

Markesh has always been Lait's closest ally; after all, that's where King Xavier was born. Our royal family has a torrid history, and the Queen, Lynette, had been through the worst of it. Her parents died tragically early on, but not before securing a marriage between the two countries.

Arla, who was used to my attempts at being grown up, just nodded. "They are. There was an incident when they arrived, and father would prefer we stay wary."

We begged her to tell us what had happened, our previous cupcake-acquiring mission forgotten as we followed her all the way back to the main parts of the castle.

"Arla!"

"Aaaaarla!!"

Eventually she snapped, twisting back around to face us both with an outstretched finger. "Both of you shut up. I'll tell you, but you need to follow me quietly back to my room."

Nodding, we excitedly trailed behind her. Eventually we reached her room, where she pulled the door open and ushered us in, a pursed finger to her lips. She closed the door as we both flopped onto the embroidered couches in her sitting room.

It was only at this point, that I realised something must have been very wrong. At sixteen, Arla was always put together, a perfect "good" girl … but right at that moment? With her blonde hair falling in front of her face and the lack of makeup, a tiredness etched across her normally fresh and spritely smile … she looked like a stranger.

Flynn, however, hadn't picked up on that.

"Arlaaaa, tell us!"

Holding up a finger to her mouth, she moved over to all the other doors in the room, closing them and then pulling the curtains shut.

Eventually, she took a deep breath and turned back to us.

"You've heard about the Written, right?" she whispered. At this point, the Written had only just started to grow in numbers. We'd been told they were out there, but nothing further than that. "The congregation had one hiding amongst their people, and when they arrived? It killed Worthy."

We both gasped – Worthy was our favourite butler.

"What?"

"No!"

Arla nods. "They swear that they didn't know, but now the King and Father are on high alert. I heard they were putting out new rules or something for the Written … to keep us safe."

Flynn looks over at me with a stupid little pout.

"Knock it off."

The blond man grins, the same smile that has won over countless women ... and men ... but has never worked on me.

"I'm sorry, Matty."

I scoff and kick my boots off, glad for a little rest, and slide into the closest chair. "Just be more present later, okay? I can't make excuses for you in front of the entire university."

Flynn nods and flops down on the couch opposite. "I still like this place."

"Really?"

"So much freedom, even with the Written."

I hear the disgust lacing his tone. "They're not all rebels," I say, shooting him a furtive glance.

Pushing locks of hair out of his face, he rolls his eyes. "Be still my beating heart, Matthew Martins, the next captain of Lait's military and my dearest friend ... a sympathiser."

Dramatic bastard.

I shrug my coat off and lob it at his head. "I'm going to have no time to lead anything if I'm stuck babysitting you forever. How about we make a deal?"

Flynn sits up, lifting the coat off his head, with an eyebrow raised. "I'm listening."

"Actually start trying during this trial period. Don't stick your dick in anything or anyone and I'll tell the King you were a good little boy who deserves to go to school."

Flynn pretends to think about it before sticking out his hand. "Deal, compadre."

I grab it and shake, certain that he'll find a problem with this place within the first week, or at the very least he'll piss off some poor unsuspecting student to the point that his father will have to send them a little monetary incentive to forget about it.

"Besides, since when do you read?"

It was only a couple of days after Arla told us about Worthy that Flynn finally admitted how he felt about the whole thing. Obviously, I knew and loved Worthy as well, but he and I were both considered

staff – Worthy wasn't the one waiting hand and foot on me.

"I'm scared, Matty."

"What about?"

"The Written that hurt Worthy."

I may not have been old enough to understand the seriousness of what was happening, but I could recognise how worried Flynn was. I reached out with my little hand and placed it on his shoulder. "You're safe here. They can't get you."

"But more of them keep coming."

Gesturing to the view outside the castle through the open window, I took a step back. "Only out there, though! Neither of us gets to leave much, but when we do, we have lots of guards trained by my dad to stop them!"

Flynn stared down at his hands. "But they got into the castle, and the guards didn't stop them then. What if they do it again? If they hurt you, or Arla, or Mother?"

I pondered why he didn't mention fear for his father.

You know how most of the time, you forget the conversations you have as a kid? Well, I've never forgotten this one. It's only one of a handful of times I've ever seen Flynn cry.

THE CLEAN

The hall is enormous, with gigantic round stone arches covering almost every wall, revealing the university grounds beyond. The openness allows the early dusk air to creep in, and I pull my general's coat closer to my chest. Not that it will do anything to stave off the brisk air though, military uniforms are made for ease of movement, not comfort ... and I'm still not used to this new one. Being a general happened so quickly after my father got sick; I was used to putting on my normal guard scrubs each day.

Knowing you'll take over the military one day, and then facing it are two very different things. Hearing that my father intends to step down soon has been weighing on me heavily. Both mother and father refuse to tell me exactly what's wrong, but the little shake in his hands and paleness of his skin indicate something bad.

Students sit in every available seat, chatting around raised tables and golden bar stools. The university hall looks more like a place to hang out than somewhere to greet the future leader of Lait. I can only imagine the disgusted look the King would have if he knew his money was being spent on this and not on something elaborate for his own entertainment.

Flynn lives like royalty and enjoys all the creature comforts of the palace, so it's clear he doesn't recognise the cash splurge.

Shifting in my spot next to him, Flynn shoots me a quick side eye as he steps up to the podium. I don't have to ask him what's wrong to know that withering look is his way of silently telling me off.

"Hello friends. My name is Flynn Bennett, even though I'm sure you're already aware of that." There is a smattering of polite laughter. "I am honoured to be staying here for the next month while I hopefully decide what to complete my postgraduate degree in. Please don't be afraid to approach me. I'm just like everyone else." I try not to cringe and roll my eyes as he winks at the group of girls closest to the stage – even though they don't seem to mind the attention of Lait's most eligible bachelor. "I look forward to really getting to know the Royal Bennett Uni life."

Gross.

As he steps back, the room bursts into a round of applause. We both wait, unsure what to do next, when the Dean steps forward. "Thank you, Prince Flynn. And on behalf of everyone here, we are so glad to have you. Now that everyone has gathered–"

The Dean's words are cut off as the double doors at the edge of the hall fling open, revealing what appears to be the university's Written contingent.

And leading them is that girl from the labs. Racking my brain for her name, I come up blank.

"Sorry, Dean Windmire, the Written weren't told about this little *meeting.*"

The room gasps as she steps forward, the group following dutifully behind her. They stop in the only part of the room that isn't occupied – directly in front of the stage.

Frances, the guard I have chosen to accompany us, steps protectively in front of Flynn, his grip firmly on his gun's safety latch. I press a hand to his chest, waiting to see what the students do. As dangerous as the Written are, I refuse to be a leader who assumes they're here for violence.

To the surprise of everyone in the room, the Written sit on the floor, some in groups and some alone, comfortably with their legs spread out. The redhead girl sits down too, her back resting against the chest of a big hulking guy who looks kind of like Flynn would if he paid more attention to the gym. I've been telling him to improve his health for ages, knowing he'll need it as he becomes King, but as he likes to put it, "Why mess with perfection?"

Telling the King that Flynn needs to work out is like talking to a blank wall, and his mother is no better, too scared to say anything that might upset him.

So that leaves me telling him to work out and hearing how he "doesn't need to" because he already has abs.

He does.

I hate it.

Some people have to work to look good.

The Dean steels himself, regathering his composure, and continues, "Of course, I apologise for the miscommunication. As I was saying, it is nearing the end of our semester, and I have organised for your final assessments to be a series of demonstrations. This will not only provide a wonderfully festive atmosphere, with all students allowed to watch, but these will also give Prince Flynn the time and opportunity to decide on what he wishes to study for his postgraduate at the beginning of next semester. When you return to your dormitories, you will find packets of information outlining your specific class demonstrations and what you have to do to prepare. Be sure to make us proud. Goodnight students."

As soon as he stops talking, the Clean students pour out of the hall, eager to get past the Written, who still sit lazily at the front. I observe the Dean move from the stage toward their seating, confronting that girl. Again, I try desperately to remember her name. Watching as she stands confidently in front of a man that I had seen scare the highest lords of the Lait court, I can't help but admire her.

Spending most of my time in the palace, I barely see Written, let alone one so brave as to stand in front of such an influential man, unwavering. Of course I've heard stories of the rebels, but there's something about her expression that lets me know she's the one in the right.

Breaking me from my daze, the Dean has returned to us once more, ushering us back to the quarters they have provided for Flynn. Despite my tiredness from the length of the day and our large trip from the first quarter, I lay awake until the early morning, my mind on that girl.

Weatherwood. The Dean had called her Weatherwood. I take a mental note to look up her file before finally succumbing to sleep.

6

Scarlett

I am furious.

One week.

The stupid university has given us only a week to attend classes and prepare for our end of semester demonstrations. I knew this whole thing was fucking unfair and unrealistic when we started, but I didn't know they'd pull something like this.

Of course, the entire thing is designed to give us an unfair disadvantage, to make us look stupid. I don't know what their end game is, and that's one of the things that annoys me the most. The Written students aren't allowed to leave the Third Quarter during the weekend and on Monday, no matter if we have an exemption or not. All the Clean students will have three more days with the professors to get ready.

As we trudge back home, Levi hears every little thing that has ever pissed me off about the entire city. (It's a long walk back to the Third Quarter.)

"Dean Windmire has been against us from the start! You saw how he looked at us when we sat down! Like we are fucking dirt on his shoe!" I grunt, words forgotten, when Levi wraps his warm arms around my waist, pulling us together. Despite his actions almost stopping me in my tracks, I can't help but enjoy the feeling of his large body enveloping mine. I silently curse him for using my massive crush against me. Not that he'd know – Levi has never looked at me twice.

I've resigned myself to the fact that I, Scarlett Weatherwood, am a smart, fiery rebel who is good to be friends with, but never anything more. I am everyone's favourite platonic buddy. I have no form of love life, and my crush on the guy that I live with doesn't help me move on. At twenty-three, going on twenty-four, I'm convinced I'll be the world's oldest virgin.

"Scar, you know we know the truth. Windmire is an old fucker who hates Written. You've just gotta ignore him."

Sighing because he's right, I mutter a weak reply under my breath, "Carry me home?"

Levi's laugh shakes through his entire chest, lightly pushing me forward. "You're hilarious as always, Scar."

Levi has adapted to the whole university thing a lot quicker than I have. Once he moved past his initial anger about being taken from the clinic, he quickly became one of the best in our little cohort.

We walk in silence the rest of the way until we finally come across the telltale signs that the Second Quarter is ending and our home is approaching. The sidewalks here are cracked, and the parks get more and more overgrown with every metre we walk. And the silence – there's something incredibly off-putting about how the Second Quarter bleeds into nothing.

Eventually we reach Smith Street, the last perimeter of the Second Quarter, a road of abandoned homes. By abandoned, I mean years and years of no inhabitants. Not one person I have ever spoken to can remember ever seeing people live along Smith. Even before the restrictions were placed on Written.

Levi runs ahead of me, his head thrown up to the sky. "Freedom!" he yells into Smith Street's void. Chuckling, I run to catch up with him.

"Shut up!" I hiss. "There could still be patrols."

Levi looks at me as if I've grown three heads. "You and I both know they never go this far." He grabs my hand, lacing our fingers together. "Come on. Almost home."

I don't think I've ever been happier to see our dilapidated little shack. Grenkwist's extra lab cleaning has really taken it out of me.

I feel like a ghost as Levi rushes me inside, both of us only just getting back in time for curfew.

The sirens start immediately as I close the door behind me, a jarring reminder of our homely prison. I trawl up to my room – on two feet, despite the strong urge to crawl from exhaustion – only to find Tilly lying on my bed, kicking her legs back and forth. With her head turned down facing the mattress, she hasn't noticed me yet.

Tilly has always wanted to be an artist, something unheard of for a Written. During my first year at the university, I started smuggling spare pieces of parchment into my bag so she had something to draw on. Looking over her shoulder now, I realise that she's busily working on her latest project. Leaning down, I whisper her name close to her ear.

"AHHHH!" she screams, flipping around and throwing her charcoal at me – don't worry, I dodged it.

"Scar! That's not fair!"

I'm sure my grin is shit-eating because I've finally gotten her back for what has been weeks of her sneaking up and scaring the absolute soul out of me. "I'd say sorry, but I'd be lying."

Tilly smirks. "Fine. I'll give you that one." She jumps off my bed to grab the charcoal, bounds back to her claimed spot and leaves some room beside her for me to collapse on my bed. I'm eager to get a look at what she's been doing, so I grab the piece of paper as she gets comfortable again next to me.

"Wow, Tills," I say, my breath catching in awe.

In stunning detail, she's been sketching me. My body is hunched over a pile of books from the university, and I'm busy scribbling in a notebook. Somehow, she's made me look serene, which I'm certain I wouldn't have been in that moment. As soon as she realises I'm snooping, she snatches the page from my hands.

"It's not finished," she huffs, and without looking at me, she jumps off the bed and stalks straight out my door.

"See ya, Tills."

I should be asleep, preparing myself and my tired legs for the long walk back to the university, but sleep feels impossible, with my mind running wild about my class demonstrations. What could they be, how will they work, and why is the university going to so much trouble? I guess that part is obvious; they want Flynn's money and the approval of the royals.

Eventually, at what I assume is around four in the morning since the sun is starting to glimmer through my thin curtains, I roll out of bed and pad down to the kitchen. Just before the entryway I stop, the voices of Levi, Zaid and Riley drifting through the thin walls. The Third Quarter is full of houses that would have been condemned if they were anywhere else, but lucky us – thin walls, thin curtains, all a reminder of our Written lower-class status.

"–Nah, Levi. That sounds a bit dangerous. You know me and Ryles aren't meant to leave Third."

"It'll be fine, Zaid! I have a pass, and I'm sure Ryles can use Scar's!"

Heat floods my body as I figure out what they are talking about. Only days after our "study" started at Royal Bennett, Levi had decided that he had the chance to play some pranks on the Clean. Most of them were harmless, and most of them had gone off without a hitch.

It was about a month ago that one had gone wrong and Levi had ended up with a gun pointed at his head. The fact that he is still trying to plan these ridiculous pranks, especially when they put us all in danger, is infuriating.

After eavesdropping a little longer, I finally get sick of listening to them and step out into the doorway, the boys falling silent. "What's going on?" I play dumb.

"Nothing Scar." My head whips over to Riley, who is sitting with his legs raised on our kitchen table. He stares at me unflinchingly, but two can play at this game.

"Oh really? That conversation didn't sound like 'nothing'..."

Zaid scoffs, his head stuck in the fridge as he looks for an early morning snack. We are lucky our fridge still works with everyone continually going in and out of it. "Just a new prank," he mutters between mouthfuls.

Levi flinches. He knows exactly how I'll react to that. I whisk around to face him, my cheeks heating with anger.

"Are you fucking kidding me, Levi? Don't you remember the last time?"

Levi waves a dismissive hand, desperate to cover over what Zaid just revealed about more pranks, even though I'm not stupid and know precisely what they were talking about. He walks over to me, wrapping an arm around my shoulders. "You trust me, right?"

Staring into his green eyes, I realise how tragically in love with my gorgeous, rebellious roommate I am. "Of course," I reply, fighting the urge to melt into his embrace.

His arm squeezes my waist, a grin lighting up his entire face. "It'll be totally fine, and I've worked out the ultimate foolproof plan." Scoffing, I pull away from him and head to the fridge.

"Whatever it is, you're not using my pass."

Riley throws me a cautionary glance before the boys start to leave for their various commitments; Riley to the markets and Zaid to visit Mia and Asher. Levi and I will need to head out shortly as well to make it back to the university on time.

The next day, no one says anything more to me regarding Levi's latest "idea", and in return I don't bring it up. They must have decided against whatever Levi's newest prank was.

At least, I hope they have.

The university didn't bother sending the Written their demonstration information, making us wait until we returned to campus today, which doesn't surprise me. Treat us like normal students … why would they? Grenkwist begrudgingly gives me half an hour alone to go over the instructions before our first tutoring session of the day.

I can't quite wrap my head around what I've read.

Written aren't allowed to leave the Third Quarter during the weekend, and the university is well aware of this.

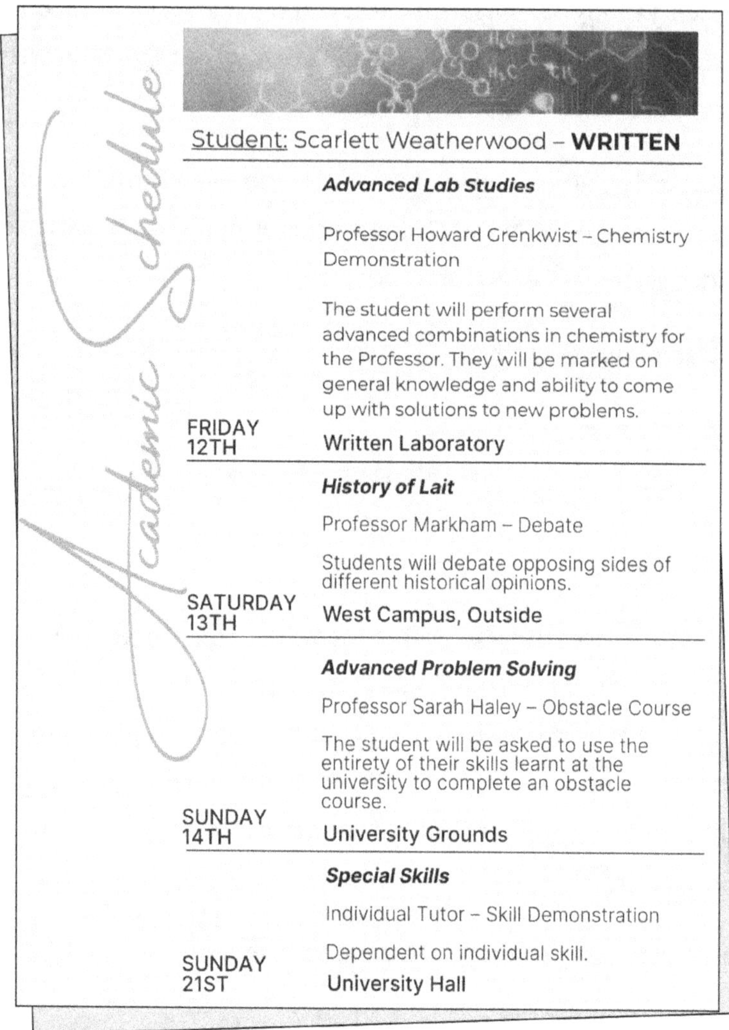

How the fuck am I meant to do three of my demonstrations?

"Miss Weatherwood. Have you finished?"

Grenkwist has plodded back out of his office to grace me with his presence. The asshole reminds me of a cat that used to live around the Third Quarter markets – only crawling out of its hole to hiss and annoy everyone and occasionally steal food.

He's balding too, just like that cat who had pulled out chunks of fur from fleas.

I choke down the slight amusement I feel at the thought of him being infested, to ask more pressing questions.

"How am I meant to do the demonstrations scheduled on weekends?"

Grenkwist smirks. "What? You don't know something? I'm shocked!"

Smug bastard.

I roll my eyes as he laughs mockingly at me. "Written have been instructed to be present on campus for the entire time that the Prince is staying."

The *entire* time? Holy shit. The university has never allowed Written in the dormitories.

"Why?"

"He's trying to learn what 'real' uni life is like, and apparently he has to do that with you people!"

You people.

Gritting my teeth, I ignore him. "Wonderful! When do I get to see my dorm?"

Grenkwist looks me up and down, disappointed at my lack of retaliation. No doubt he would have loved to punish me again. "Right now. University officials have asked first-period professors to take the Written students to their accommodations."

I practically skip to the door because this news has to really piss him off. He growls as he follows behind me. Just like that damn cat. "Ground rules. You stay close by, and you don't enter anywhere I haven't expressly granted you permission to. You don't talk to anyone, and you sure as hell don't make any kind of scene."

Sighing as he sees his attempt at scaring me has failed, he unlocks the door and, without another word, he turns right down the hallway.

7

Matthew

If I have to pull Flynn away from flirting with one more student, I'm going to suggest to his father that he be castrated. All morning he has spent going back and forth between hordes of people that want to meet the famous Prince. You'd think after three days that everyone would have had their fill, but no, Flynn is too remarkably charming for his own fucking good. Today is one of those days when I miss the shy boy that only used to flirt ... terribly ... with my sister.

Surveying from across the courtyard, I watch as he slings an arm across the shoulders of a gorgeous blonde girl and winks at her friend.

All they do is laugh.

Go figure. If I, or any other normal human, were to be that much of a man-whore, we'd get punched. But no, as always, Flynn gets away with murder. It is only occasionally that I allow myself to think of Flynn as my friend, and this isn't one of those times. Right now, this is job time.

It's a flash of red hair that catches my eye, pulling me away from Flynn's grotesque display. Weatherwood. Or Scarlett, as I'd since read in her profile. Frustratingly, there is very little to know about her ... the file was sparse. She hadn't crossed my mind until now, watching her follow behind that professor from the labs. My first instinct that day had been to scoff at the man; he seemed uptight, and I could only imagine how he treated Written when they were alone.

Scarlett Weatherwood is twenty-three years old and has been at the university for a year, and there is something about her I just can't shake. Her limited profile only adds fuel to the fire, and for reasons unbeknownst to me, I want to know details.

This isn't good. My job is to protect Flynn, not to become obsessed with someone who is perhaps dangerous. That night at the club flashes in my mind, my knife lodged in the back of someone that looked oddly similar.

Shaking away my thoughts, I divert my attention back over to Flynn and snort. My friend has his nose stuck in the blonde's hair, and his hand is raking lower and lower on her back. Rolling my eyes, I decide that is enough for the ridiculous public display of affection – for both Flynn's reputation and my stomach lining –

and walk over.

"Your Highness, you are due in the northern building in ten minutes."

Flynn is clearly pissed, but it's nothing I haven't handled before. "Mister Martins, I do believe I can find my way over there in time."

Mirroring every filthy and annoyed look I've ever seen my father do, I shoot the two girls a glare, both of them reading it as their cue to leave.

Flynn throws his hands up as he watches them leave. "What the fuck, man!" I roll my eyes and place a firm hand on his shoulders, guiding him from the courtyard. As we round a secluded corner away from the students that had gathered, I stop.

"Do you not remember the conversation we had three days ago?"

Flynn rubs his shoulder, glaring at me. "No. I tend to zone out when you start yelling."

It is at this point I have to remind myself that adult Matthew is not allowed to punch the Crown Prince. As much as I want to ... and I really want to.

Taking a deep breath, I put my hand on his shoulder. "You're here to work, to study. You know your dad is just going to make you go back home as soon as he catches a whiff of your, shall we say ... 'escapades'?"

Flynn nods. Any mention of his dad always does wonders to sober him up. "I'll be a good little prince."

Why am I not allowed to punch him?

Finally, the first day of demonstrations starts and provides me with a bounty of students to keep Flynn entertained for the day. Let's call it an unintentional rest day. My favourite days at the palace are when Flynn has to sit in on his father's council. He hates it, but I love not having to play babysitter for the afternoon.

The morning passes with little to no action, and soon enough we are herded back towards the Written laboratories. Flynn tenses up beside me as soon as he realises the direction we are headed. Placing a hand on his shoulder, I whisper words of encouragement in his ear. Not including the incident at the bar, King Xavier's attitude has really done a number on Flynn, and his fear surrounding the Written means he shuts down every single time.

Ever since Worthy was murdered, King Xavier's fear of the Written has grown, and the more prejudiced he became, the more Flynn has been affected having to sit there all day and listen to him over the years. The King never considers that his son is one day going to be the ruler of Lait, including the Written that live here, and at the moment ... well, Flynn can hardly be in the same room as them.

He brushes me off. "I'm fine. Back off!"

He isn't fine. But I wouldn't know that, would I? Not from having been his best friend since we were kids. Stubborn fuck.

We reach the Written side of campus. The Written laboratories aren't like the main campus ones. The lights here are dimmer, and I swear the thermostat is set at least a couple of degrees lower.

I remember when they announced the Written program; it was only a couple of days in before they realised they needed to split the Clean and Written cohorts because of the fear and unrest of the Clean students. A shiver runs down my spine as I remember the students who were killed, and I thank the god I don't believe in that Flynn wasn't here.

I ignore the little uptick in my heart when I see we are being led to the same place that intriguing Written girl was only a couple of days ago. Ushering us through the door, the Dean puts a hand on my shoulder. "Be extra vigilant in here, Martins. Scarlett Weatherwood is a handful. She's also a possible associate of a group on campus that likes to take part in some incredibly dangerous pranks. Don't be surprised if they try something today."

I nod and push past him, annoyed but maintaining my composure. Everyone knows who my father is, so they should know that I can do my job. Why does it feel like I spend most of my life proving that I am halfway competent? Competent for my dad, for the King, for

Flynn. If proving myself to them is one of my biggest problems, how will I ever prove myself to Lait?

In one corner of the room, they have set up what appears to be a viewing area, and at this stage it sits full of dignitaries. Clearly, no one is opting to go to a Written demonstration unless obligated. A couple of other Written students sit scattered in the handful of seats the university bothered to put out, most of them shrinking at Flynn's arrival. Without the immediate presence of the red-headed Written girl, they appear to have lost their nerve. A couple of professors stand huddled around another table off to the side, a lab bench taking up centre stage in the room.

One professor steps up in front of the lab bench to address the room.

"Hello students, and my warmest greetings to Prince Flynn. I am so honoured that the university has chosen lab subjects to be among the first for the demonstrations. Whilst these demonstrations are from Written students, I can assure you of a high quality of work, and hopefully an educating experience."

Huh?

I rack my brain, sieving through everything I've ever been taught about Written, none of which included anything about any mental decline. Shifting in my seat, I run through countless hours of lessons I've attended.

Written are dangerous.

THE CLEAN

Written need to stay in the Third Quarter.

Three plus designations makes someone a "fully fledged" Written.

But *mental decline?*

Nope. Nothing. Not once in my years of tutoring has it been said that long-term designations cause problems intellectually. So why the fuck is this guy acting like the Written students are dumb?

It's not long before the first Written student steps up, a man who appears to be much older than the rest of the Written cohort. His mentor stands in front of the bench, instructing him on what to make. Three professors sit off to the side, each studying small screens that show his work up close.

"Now please use the created formulas together as a new method of your own original design."

The Written man's eyes widen, the telltale sign of when somebody smart doesn't know what to do. This last instruction has stumped him. After a short time fussing over his bench, he leaves the room, his design sitting on the table for the scrutiny of the professors – a concoction of black goop resembling something awful, and the putrid smell wafts over to where we sit. The judges shake their heads as they get up to inspect it in person.

Another three students go through the tests, each of them getting stuck on that final question. It seems like none of them prepared for what is required – it feels really unusual that so many are getting stumped. Are they not as prepared for this as the Clean students? Or maybe the mental decline thing is real. As the day drags on, my eyes get heavier and heavier, until the next student captures my attention.

Scarlett Weatherwood.

She looks completely different from what I'd seen the other day. Instead of eyes wide and hair flying all over her face, this woman looks perfectly put together and focussed. Her red hair is slicked back into a tight bun, and her lab coat looks so white I would swear she has never worn it before. Unlike the other students, she takes every instruction with a polite nod of her head and an assured look on her face. I watch on intently as she approaches the last question that has stumped the others.

"Now please use the created formulas together as a new method of your own original design."

Scarlett crooks her head to the side. "A formula for anything?"

My eyes widen. She's the first one to speak during her demonstration, and as I peep around at the people sitting next to me, I realise all of them look as shocked as I do.

Scarlett's instructor, Grenkwist, is the only one who doesn't bat an eye. With a brief nod, Scarlett's eyes shoot back down to her workstation, confidence returning just like it had before. I watch in awe as her time ticks down until eventually she stops, capping a bottle and handing it to Grenkwist.

"A burn-healing solution."

Scarlett turns and leaves the room, and suddenly every single judge looks more interested than they have all day. Grenkwist walks the bottle over to their table, setting it down and allowing them to examine it. One judge asks for a slab of fake skin to be brought out. I ignore the lurch in my stomach. The future general of the King's army should not be so weak, but I am only human, and "fake skin"? Gross. Why that even exists is beyond me.

Fighting the urge to close my eyes, I watch as they hold a Bunsen burner to the slab, the fake skin blistering like actual skin would. Acrid smoke rises, and I stifle my disgust as a waft of burnt flesh makes its way over to where Flynn and I sit. The only thing missing is the appearance of a designation. What appears to be the most senior of the judges uncorks the bottle and begins drizzling the liquid onto the charred skin. I remain rigid in my chair, fighting the urge to stand and see the results.

Could Scarlett really be the first to produce something useful out of today's demonstrations?

In front of me, the Dean stands up and walks over to the judge's table. His eyes widen, and I catch whispers of the conversation.

"She actually–"

"How long–"

"–she should be training with someone better than Howard

Grenkwist."

With the last sentence, they nod in unison.

Eventually, the Dean turns back towards us, walking up to Flynn.

"Your Highness, that concludes these demonstrations. Please enjoy the rest of your day on campus." Without further ado, the Dean sweeps from the room, his fellow teachers following close behind. The Dean has been wanting to stick to Flynn like glue since day one, so his quick departure is both out of character and out of royal protocol.

"Well, that was weird."

I turn to Flynn. "You noticed too?"

He shrugs. "It was a bit hard not to."

Sitting back in my chair, trying to get comfortable, I sigh, "So! What debauchery do I have to keep you from for the rest of the day?"

Without even looking at him, I know the pompous bastard is smirking.

"Do you think there's any kind of party on campus?" Flynn asks.

I snort, the real ugly kind of amused. It's Friday night at a college. Of course there's gonna be a fucking party somewhere.

"You're right, stupid question. I wonder where the best one is?"

I follow him as he gladly flees the Written building, my mind still on Scarlett. My dread grows with every step. Whatever this is? I need to stop.

Hopefully, I won't see her again.

8

Scarlett

The oldest dorm on campus – where they'd stuck us Written for the duration of the demonstrations – is also where the coolest of the Royal Bennett students hold their stupid weekly ragers. The building has been abandoned for a couple years ... the perfect place to make us feel right at home.

I groan, burying my head under my pillow as the music only seems to get louder. From the moment I'd been escorted back from the first demonstration, I could hear the bass. Who the fuck do they think they are? Didn't they have demonstrations to prepare for? I laugh to myself, a bitter taste on my tongue. Their lives don't hang in the balance if they fail. This is all just harmless university fun for them.

When I was younger, I spent a lot of time pondering what it

would be like to be a Clean. The freedoms I could have, what it might feel like to grow up with parents that cared more about their daughter than the words scrawled on her body. Torture, it was always torture, but all Written did it.

My parents had dropped me off at the Third Quarter gate when I turned eleven. Why I spent so much time thinking about something I could never have is beyond me. Then, when the Royal Bennett University initiative started, and I had exposure to the rest of Lait as an adult, I realised how stupid I was being. The Clean are vain and petty; they party and don't have to worry about where their next meal comes from. Why would I want to be something with no substance? Even if no substance meant having a better quality of life.

The university's rejected beds, which feel like sleeping on cardboard, exacerbate my sleep deprivation. Eventually, I decide that I have to confront the pompous pricks downstairs. Stupid decision, yes. Sleep deprived? Probably.

Down the stairs I go, my glamorous outfit of an oversized t-shirt and shorts completely forgotten. Clean students pack the hallway, making out, drinking, and from what I can see through an open door, fucking. As they realise what I am – it comes in handy sometimes – I have a clear path made for me, right through the middle. My filthy "Written" status parts them like the Red Sea. It also helps that they can see my legs, and my designations clear as day. Conversation dies off as I strut up to what seems to be the epicentre of the whole shebang. A closed door with an inconspicuous note on the front ... sarcasm, darlings ... the note says, "Party Here!"

"I don't think you're meant to be here." A blonde girl attempts to stop me, placing herself between me and the door. Her friends pull her back, but evidently she's full on liquid courage. Looking down at her barely-there singlet, I can't help but wonder what it would be like to feel comfortable showing that much skin in public.

"Whose party is this?" I snap at her. I've dealt with people like this for an entire year ... I'm used to being treated like patient zero of the next plague.

"Harry Brandt," the girl spits in return. I push her aside, and she recoils as my hand touches her. Her friends look mortified.

Gritting my teeth, I push open the door. I'm not surprised to see that this room is just as full of people as the hallway is. Half of the university has shown up to ruin my sleep. In the middle of the room stands a table covered in red plastic cups.

Royal Bennett University doesn't beat any stereotypes.

"I'm looking for Harry Brandt," I yell out into the crowd.

A couple of people finally look over at me and gasp, their conversations forgotten. Peering around the room, my eyes fall on the speaker that is the source of my current problems.

Three forceful strides and the speaker cord is in my hand.

THE CLEAN

SCREEEEECHHHH!

For the first time in existence, the sound of something being unceremoniously unplugged is the most satisfying thing I've ever heard. Now I have the attention of the entire room.

"There are people trying to sleep. Kindly fuck off and find somewhere else to party."

Everyone looks around at each other, lost for words. No one knows what to do, and to be honest? I kind of like it.

"Why should we?"

Surely the mysterious voice has to be Brandt. "You listen–" I wheel around, stopping in my tracks as I realise who has spoken.

Prince Flynn.

Crown *fucking* Prince Flynn.

With his head held high, he saunters over to me, the type of swagger that only comes from pompous pricks that have everything they have ever wanted handed to them on a silver platter. I recoil as he gets close enough that I can smell his breath; he is undoubtedly hammered. Getting right in my face, he looks down at me. "Why should we move for some scummy little Written?"

I clench my fist as the people around him murmur in agreement. "This scummy little Written is a student here, and like everyone else, needs to sleep."

"I thought Written didn't need sleep!"

"Yeah! Don't you drink blood or something?"

I stand there as the chorus of drunken idiots tells me every myth I've ever heard about the Written, and believe me, there are a lot. Steeling myself, I stare Flynn down.

"Turn down the music."

Flynn takes a step back, raising his hands in mock surrender. "Okay! Fine!" He walks over to the speaker, plugging it back in. As the music starts again, I turn towards the door.

Then I stop.

The fucker has made it louder.

My nostrils flare as I look back to where Flynn stands, a sly and dismissive smile creeping across his face. Cursing under my breath, I decide that retreat is the only option. My eyes are glued to the ground as everyone I pass makes jabs at me, as if the Prince has given them permission.

At the end of the hallway, when I finally break free of the crowd, someone grabs my arm.

"I'm sorry about him."

I turn around, ready to give whoever this is a piece of my mind.

No doubt they will decide to abuse me in some way as well. Then I take in what he's wearing. Racking my brains, I finally remember the uniform. It's Royal Military. And the bluest eyes I've ever seen … military man. The asshole from the lab a few days ago.

Hitting his hand away, I take a step back. "What? You're sorry he didn't take it further? Didn't bend me over to see if Written really are just sluts?"

Military man sighs and pushes his hair back. He would be really pretty if not for the continuous frown and the general unpleasant personality. "No, Miss Weatherwood, I mean, I'm sorry about him and what he said."

Taking a step back, I gauge what his deal is. "Well … Thanks, I guess."

Nodding, military man smooths his hands on his jacket. "He's drunk and says stupid things."

Shaking my head, I look down at my feet. "It's nothing I haven't heard from completely sober people in the daylight as well."

"I–"

Taking another step backward, I gesture for him to stop. "You've done your duty, okay? I don't need false sympathy. Go back to your Prince."

I'm so tired I don't even realise he somehow knew my last name.

9

Matthew

Why is my heart in my throat? Desperation floods through me, and I want to chase after her and assure her that his behaviour was out of line. Royal privilege be damned. Despite the King's own beliefs about the Written, he would have been appalled to see what Flynn did. The one thing that King Xavier cares more about than anything else is image, and the future king acting like a pig, even to a Written? It doesn't look good. Instead, I stand and watch as she turns on her heel and leaves up the stairs.

Scarlett Weatherwood is starting to be someone that can't be ignored, and that bothers me.

Huffing, I walk back towards Flynn, who has decided that going back and forth between making out with Harry Brandt and several other girls is acceptable behaviour for the future king. I make a mental note to send an envoy to his father. I'm sure that a brief message from the King will stop this nonsense, at least for a little while.

Reaching out, I grab the back of his shirt, ignoring the indignant response from a hot blonde as I pull him towards me.

"You are a child."

"And you're a fucking cockblock! Go annoy someone else!"

Rolling my eyes, I look down at him. "You are an insufferable drunk."

His bloodshot eyes stare back, blond hair stuck in all directions. "Seriously. Go away."

Shaking my head, I force him to take another step back, further away from temptation. "I'm doing my job, Flynn. Remember? Future leader of the military and your personal guard?"

Shooting me a sly smile, he puts a hand on my chest. "Who does the military leader report to?"

"The King."

"Who's the *future* King?"

"Well, you."

I stumble as he pushes me backwards. "And as the future leader of the military, your future King is who you answer to, yes?"

Fuck.

His smile widens even further. "As your *future* King, I demand you fuck off and mind your own business."

Flynn has never been an easy person to understand, and during these first days at Royal Bennett, that has been ever apparent. Trust me, he wasn't always like this, but his story isn't mine to tell. Unfortunately, his life is mine to clean up, and that's exactly what I find myself doing the very next morning, ushering two hungover students from his room. Arla would have laughed her head off at the little blond boy who blushed at her presence, now turning into Lait's resident man-whore.

Breathing a sigh of relief, I brace myself against the back of the door after finally getting Harry Brandt out of the room. Flynn is going to do my head in, especially as I seem to be the one that has to field the questions from his father about why he hasn't settled down yet with a beautiful bride. Walking into his room, I pray he isn't still naked. Yes, he's my best friend, and I should have more faith, but this isn't my first rodeo.

The urge to gag is strong as he stretches, laid out on the generously sized bed – definitely not typical college size – with a white sheet perched precariously over his hips. Unfortunately for my job, Flynn is a very good-looking guy, and the bastard knows it too.

"Good morning, Matty," he groans.

Ignoring him and walking straight towards the window, I throw the blinds open, the morning sunshine flooding the room and causing Flynn to curse me. It's so worth it as I cheerfully say, "Hello sunshine."

Shooting me a million different hand gestures, he removes the sheet, revealing himself to me. "You slimy fucker."

Cursing back and muttering a quick plea for decency, I hide my face. Flynn just smiles, not a care in the world.

I walk over to where his clothes have been haphazardly thrown, picking them up one by one and throwing them at his head. I scoff as I pick up the lacy bra his female companion must have left behind.

Leaving the room and hoping that Flynn will come out shortly and dressed, I pick up the folder the Dean had prepared with his timetable.

There is only one demonstration today.

A debate.

Wonderful.

The university has scheduled a debate to be attended by a prince with the world's smallest attention span. And I can't say I'm excited to have to sit in a room for this, especially after being stuck watching boring lab demonstrations yesterday. I hear a shower start and end, and before long, Flynn comes waltzing out of his room. Life is not cutting me any slack.

"So," he says, stretching, eyes still half closed. "What's on for today, Matty?"

Throwing the binder down and walking over to him, I place a hand on his shoulder. "Your absolute favourite…" I grin. "A fucking debate."

Now, I can't say that I take great pleasure in messing with the Prince, because that would be against my position. But I can say that I take the utmost pleasure in wiping the annoying look off my best friend's face, and luckily for me, Flynn fits that category too.

The debates are held on a side of campus that neither of us has been to before. It's green and lush, with plants and foliage everywhere, as if we've stepped into the world's largest greenhouse. Except this greenhouse is in the middle of Lait's most prestigious university and full of people that are still half drunk from the night before.

I'm glad for the fresh air, though. It might help me stay awake.

Even Flynn, who famously never gets hungover, trails behind me in the largest pair of sunglasses I have ever seen him wear. The next time he feels the tiniest bit better, I am never going to let him live it down.

"Ah, fuck. Why's it so bright?"

"The outdoors, Mister Bennett, tends to be like this."

If looks could kill, the university would be collecting my body right then and there. It's a wonderful start to the day. Even with glasses, the scowl I see plastered on Flynn's face is epic.

Soon, a stage and seating area come into view, rows and rows of chairs set out. It's clear that this is a Clean subject; the chairs are too well looked after. I can't help but sigh in relief; less danger and less need for me to be on my toes.

The seats fill surprisingly fast for a debate, with rows and rows of chatting students teeming into the area. For once, Flynn isn't tempted to go off and find anyone to flirt with, his headache keeping him confined to the uncomfortable plastic chair in the front.

"Why a debate? Do they want me to die?"

Ignoring him, I keep my view straight at the stage as the first set of students steps up.

"Hello, my name is Tahlia, and I will be speaking for the affirmative side."

"And my name is Isaac. I will argue against."

A professor stands between them. "Your topic is, 'The government should have divided Lait into four equal parts.'"

This is going to be a very long and incredibly boring day.

It's just as the sun crests the horizon that the day gets interesting. At least ten Written students walk toward the stage, most of them taking a seat on the grass. Then, one by one, they come onstage, debating against Clean students. Flabbergasted, I look over at Flynn, who sits there with his mouth agape, just as confused as I am.

"I didn't think they interacted," Flynn leans over, whispering in my ear. "I was told I wouldn't have to go near them."

Recognising the impending panic attack, I turn to him. "I'm sure there's a perfectly valid reason. I'll speak with the Dean later."

Both of us shift our attention back towards the stage as a loud round of chatter breaks out amongst the crowd of students. Quickly scanning for something amiss, I can't see anything out of the ordinary until I realise they are talking about the Written student that has jumped onto the stage.

It's the guy I've seen with Scarlett, the more muscular version of Flynn. He's taken his jacket off, revealing a tank top with low sides. That explains the crowd's outburst.

Whilst there are no specific laws about what Written wear while in the company of Clean, there are expectations, and Scarlett's friend has swept them out the window with one small action.

BROKEN. TWISTED. DAMAGED. INTERNAL BLEEDING.

They are some of the biggest designations I've ever seen. My father had taught me about the Written and had mentioned that the severity of the cause will increase or decrease the size, but I've never seen designations like this.

"My name is Levi Smith, and I will argue for."

The crowd breaks into another round of murmurs while I make a mental note of his surname to search up his file later. Another Written man steps up and walks over to the other podium. This one is dressed in the more typical long sleeves and pants.

"My name is Thaddeus Michael, and I will argue against."

This must be the first time they have ever put two Written onstage at the same time, and it's clearly making everyone uncomfortable. Even I'm on edge. A professor I had seen earlier steps forward with an unusual look on his face.

"Your debate topic is, 'The restrictions put on Lait's Written population are just and fair, and for the good of Lait as a society.'"

The colour drains out of both the Writtens' faces.

Thaddeus splutters, "Excuse me?"

I've only seen Smith once, and for most of that time I was focused on trying to figure out Scarlett, but his subsequent behaviour seems out of character. Redness inches up his neck, his face flushing.

"You want me to argue *for* the abuse of Lait citizens?" he growls.

The crowd erupts into an outraged conversation. The professor stands calmly and raises a sure hand towards the crowd.

"Quiet down. Mr Smith is clearly confused."

He turns towards Levi. "Written are a part of Lait history and thus form a part of this curriculum. A third-party creates the debate topics and assigns roles at random. You must argue for whichever question is assigned."

You don't have to be a psychology major to see that Smith is furious.

"Okay." His disbelief is clear, and he stands as if poised to tackle the man.

The professor turns back towards the crowd. "We'll start, as always, with the affirmative."

Flynn nudges me on the shoulder, worry etched across his face. "How is this allowed?"

"I don't know," I whisper, watching Levi try to keep his emotions under control.

Gripping the edge of the platform in front of him, he begins.

"The sanctions that have been put on the Written population are for the good of Lait because..." he pauses; everyone can see how hard it is for him to continue, despite their preconceived notions of the Written. "Because why should Clean citizens have to be around us? Don't you deserve better? After all, aren't we all dangerous?"

I look around as the crowd shifts in their seats, everyone giving each other confused looks. Where is he going with this?

"What are the Written if not considered second-class citizens? God forbid Lait has to help those most in need. Let's not forget how filthy they ... *we* ... are!"

Some of the more confident students start yelling their opinions.

"Fuck off!"

"You deserve it!"

My hand drifts down to the gun at my side. This is going south, and fast. The professor steps forward again, attempting to subdue the crowd. "That's enough. Let him finish." But Levi barely gives the professor time to regain control over the crowd before continuing.

"The thing that the Clean love to forget is that they could become a Written at any time. Do you know what it's like to see children abandoned by their parents at the Third Quarter divide because of some drawings on their skin? Because, god forbid, they have a condition that is completely out of their control?"

Two guards beeline through the crowd towards Levi, but he's not fazed. If anything, passion erodes at his voice, erring on the side of hysteria.

"Do you know what it's like to try and make a good life for yourself when most of your country wants you dead? I work at the only medical centre in the Third Quarter. We barely have enough to help with the smallest of problems. Many of us are starving and die before reaching middle age."

The professor raises a hand towards the guards, stopping them within an arm's reach of Levi. It eludes me why he seems so dead set on letting him finish his points.

"I met a thirteen-year-old girl last week who was new to the Third Quarter. She'd been in the medical centre for about a month because her injuries were so bad. This girl became a Written ... because she was *raped*."

The crowd gasps, and my stomach lurches. Levi can no longer contain his fury.

"THIS GIRL BECAME A WRITTEN BECAUSE SOME DISGUSTING BASTARD TOOK AWAY HER INNOCENCE!" Tears stream down his face, but his voice remains strong.

"How could you be okay with that? What is the good of Lait if anyone who doesn't have enough money to get their designations removed becomes the dirt of society? She's a child, and I guarantee you that raping fucker is walking around out here just fine, waiting to do it again with another innocent person, with all the money and all the food he could ever need. What sort of country abandons its citizens that are most in need?"

He pauses, considering his final words.

"Fuck Lait." He throws his hands to the crowd, giving everyone two middle fingers.

And that's when all hell breaks loose.

10

Scarlett

How I ended up running late for my debate, I have no clue. Throwing books into my bag with one hand, I quickly shove the minuscule bit of food the university has left in our common area for breakfast down my throat with the other.

"Help!"

My head snaps up, and I rush towards the shout, my bag forgotten on the floor. Four of my fellow students crowd around the open door, and I have to squint past the sudden rush of sunlight to figure out who they are. Then I see him.

Levi's tall, muscular figure drapes over Thaddeus Michael, as the older man struggles to pull him along. My hands shake as my feet stand planted in the hallway. "What ... wha ...?"

The group pushes past me, bringing Levi into the common area. Snapping out of my haze, with one sweep I follow them and clear the table so Thaddeus can put him down.

Levi mumbles under his breath as he lies on the table, his left hand clutching his side. I resist the urge to gag as I note his injuries. There's so much blood, and it's soaking through Levi's torn and battered tank top. What was he thinking wearing this to the debates? His designations are visible, or at least they were. It looks like they've been ripped or scratched off by the amount of red I'm seeing. Blood also seeps from an open wound across his eyebrow, and his jaw is already forming a bruise the size of my hand. His eyelids flutter as he sweeps in and out of consciousness.

Thaddeus stands silent next to me, watching as the two girls that were with him rush around, boiling water and ripping apart clothes for bandages. The invisible hand of every Written's demise is already working its way across his skin – Levi's first face designations.

"What happened?"

Thaddeus, usually quiet and solemn, displays unexpected emotion. He chokes back tears as he recounts what took place. "That professor, Marshall, I think? He set us up." Thad takes a step forward towards Levi. "He gave us a fucking stupid debate question, trying to get us to say something incriminating. Levi gave him exactly what he wanted."

Fuck.

"What was the debate topic?"

"Something about justifying why Lait is so clever to treat Written like shit."

My heart drops in my chest. Out of all the possible topics, it was Levi who had gotten the thing he was most passionate about, most hot-headed. It's easy to imagine some of the things he could have said.

Thad looks back at me. "Did he tell you about the girl?"

"No?"

The older man sighs. "I didn't realise that Levi had been put on that case, otherwise I would have stopped him sooner."

"What happened? What girl?"

"One of his patients at the clinic. Someone raped her and then abandoned her at the border."

My hands shake, and my blood boils. Of course Levi would react like that. What human couldn't see how wrong this all was? But then, with everything I know and learn about the Clean, it's easy to see them removed from their humanity.

One of the girls who has been helping stem the bleeding in Levi's side looks at me funny as my head droops into my hands, falling asleep at the table Levi lies on.

"Get some rest. I can stay here," she says kindly.

Shaking my head, I sit up, rolling my shoulders. "You've done enough. I can look after him."

After one last sideways glance, the girl leaves. Looking down at Levi, I suppress the urge to retch. We had done our best to bandage and clean his side, but blood still seeps through. I find his forehead clammy as I reach my hand up to check his temperature. He'd fallen asleep a couple of hours earlier, thankfully. His screams as they poured alcohol on his side will haunt me forever.

The floorboards don't warn me that someone else being around. Ever since we'd been living here, they've creaked. It's only when someone swears quietly in the hall that I realise I'm not alone.

"*Fuck.*"

I scramble up from the table, wondering if my eyes look as huge as they feel, bugging out of my head from shock. Putting a defensive hand out in front of me, I take a step forward toward the visitor.

I'm not trained to fight, but there's no way this dickhead in a uniform is taking Levi.

"You're not taking him."

Military man shakes his head. "I ... I'm not going to take him."

Exhausted, I drop my hands. If this pretty boy wants to cause trouble, I have no energy left to stop him. "What are you doing here, then?"

Military man shifts in the doorway, looking uncomfortable, as he should. He pauses before whispering, "I don't know."

It happens unexpectedly, but I can't help myself when a laugh escapes my lips at the absurdity of it all as I slump back down on the stool next to Levi. "Man of few words."

He leans against the doorframe, looking just as tired as I am.

"I was at the debate when it happened."

My head perks up at that. "What?"

He nods. "Why would he lie like that? Your friend. Why would he lie?"

Resisting the urge to roll my eyes, I look back at him. "Even though I don't know all the details, I can assure you ... Levi doesn't lie."

Military man raises an eyebrow. "He doesn't lie? Everyone lies."

"Not about stuff like that … things he's so passionate about."

Military man hums, his eyes drifting back towards Levi's unconscious form. "Why hasn't he seen a nurse?"

Is this guy serious? I sit up and gesture to the rundown hellhole around me. "Look at this place. It's barely fit for the rats, let alone humans. You really think they care whether he dies?"

It's only the small raise of his eyebrow that tells me I've caught him off guard. "It may not appear like it from the coziness of the castle, but this is our life."

He steps into the room, his eyes taking in how shitty our student accommodations are. "This is … I … I'm sorry."

Throwing my hands up, I jump back off the stool and walk towards him, hoping the closeness scares him off. Like it does for most people when a Written gets too near. This time, though? It doesn't. Military man stays planted on the spot. Getting closer to his face, I coolly retort, "What are you sorry for? There's nothing you can do except enjoy your carefree castle life."

From this angle, I can see his eyes in more detail. If he were anyone else, I would point out just how blue they are. With my hands on my hips, I remain standing here, waiting for him to say something … anything.

"Argh!" We are quickly snapped back into the real world, where Levi, who has rolled on his side, has his hands grasped over the site of his major wound. "Fuuuuuck!" he moans.

Running back over to him, I grab at his hands, pulling them away, fearing he's caused more damage. His skin feels searing hot. I'm so worried about the infection that appears to be setting in.

"What hurts?"

Levi struggles before quietly answering, "Fucking everything."

I look over to where Military man stands to tell him to leave. If he's not going to help, then we don't need him around.

But he's already gone.

11

Matthew

I feel like a fucking coward as I turn away from helping her, leaving her friend to writhe in pain, but I'm already on thin ice just by being there alone, I can't risk anyone seeing and for reasons unbeknownst to me, I trust Scarlett Weatherwood not to blow my cover.

My brain runs a million miles an hour as I make my way back towards Flynn's rooms.

How is it possible that they could leave him like that? I'd watched as Smith's friends dragged him out of the area. A large group of security personnel contained the brawl, and I focused on keeping Flynn's head down to ensure his safety. Even as Lait's next head of military, public brawls like this were out of my scope for now, my only focus being to ensure the future king's safety.

But what I witnessed today has left me rattled.

My whole life has been about the military helping people. That was the whole reason Lait citizens joined the guard and, in turn, the army, because from a young age we are told that the reason for the military existing is to help. That is all Father has ever said to me … "The military are the helpers. They're the saviours." Obviously he's blowing smoke, trying to make his job sound more important than it is, and even as a kid I knew that, but I still signed up to the ideal.

Father wasn't the first person to tell me that, though. The first person was the King, so I've always gathered there is at least a bit of truth in what my father has instilled in me, because after all, why would the King lie?

Over and over, I ruminate on the state of Levi, his bruised face and that god-awful deep cut on his side. These were submission techniques taught for Lait's enemies, not its citizens … Written or Clean. Why would general guards know them? And why would they have used them in this circumstance? I would hardly consider an out-of-control debate among university students to be a life or death situation. None of them were armed.

Knocking on Flynn's bedroom door, I wait a moment before pushing my way in, his decency be damned.

"What the fuck, man?"

We've barely been at Royal Bennett for a week, and I've already seen Flynn's dick a handful of times. My hands fly up to cover my eyes as he springs up from the bed, quickly pulling on a pair of boxers.

"You can open your eyes now," Flynn says, deadpanning me.

Slowly, I pull my hands from my eyes. "I think I'm traumatised."

Flynn grins, walking towards me. "You've seen it before."

"Worst day of my life."

"Why? I've even offered to show you how well I use it."

I shove him away playfully. "Besides the fact that I've repeatedly told you I don't swing that way, I'm also not interested in contracting every STD under the sun."

Flynn sits back down on the edge of the bed, a hand on his bare chest. "I'm clean, thank you very much."

Shaking my head, I refrain from making any further jokes. "I need to talk to you."

Flynn flops back, his blond hair fanning around his head, closing his eyes. "Hit me."

"Promise?"

Getting up on his elbows and looking at me, he raises a concerned eyebrow. "Are we joking right now, or are you playing fully serious, overprotective, bodyguard Matty?"

I ignore him. "Is it true how little medical help we send to the Third Quarter?"

Flynn falls back again, huffing. "It's not really my job, Matty, but yes, Father only sends envoys every four months."

I move closer to him and look down, meeting his eyes. "But do we send doctors? Nurses?"

"I don't know."

There it is. Flynn doesn't know. He never does. I berate myself for even bothering to ask. Flynn hates official business and does everything in his power to avoid it. Flynn eyes me curiously, and I'm sure he notices the way my shoulders slump as I move back towards the door. As I twist the handle, he stops me.

"Wait … do you think it's true what that guy said? About the girl?"

"I don't know."

They put the demonstrations on hold for a week after the debate shitshow. A day passes, and I can't let go of the image of Levi Smith writhing in pain on that old kitchen table. My training had kicked in instantly when I was talking to Scarlett, my eyes drifting over the meagre amount of medical equipment they had – if you could call wrapped rags and boiled water "medical equipment".

It's only after I take a wrong turn upon leaving the breakfast hall that I decide to do something stupid, and something my father will lose his shit over if he ever finds out.

The medical cupboard has been left wide open as a call for help comes over the nurses' division speakers. Painkillers ... sitting there ... easy to grab, right? Surely, I can't be blamed? I'm just a guard doing my duty and helping the citizens of Lait ... if my duty is to steal and provide unsanctioned goods to the Written.

Berating myself, I slip the bottle into my pocket and move on, nodding solemnly at any medical students who run past. Am I really planning to go back there? Levi has a record; I'd seen it after I got curious last night. Would it really matter if he succumbed to his wounds? One less problem for us.

Don't be a dick.

Don't you love the little voices in your head?

This is insane.

He's still human.

What if you get caught?

Just tell them you were scouting the area for threats.

What if she's there?

Fuck.

The worst thing that little voice can do is be right, and this time, as much as I go back and forth, it is. My "interest" in Scarlett Weatherwood is impacting my ability to carry through my duty as a guard to Flynn. I'm finding myself more and more distracted by the clever, sharp redheaded girl. But there's a bigger issue here, and that is my duty as the future head of the Lait military.

A future where we are meant to help.

12

Scarlett

His fever has significantly worsened overnight, and I can't help the nagging feeling that whatever kind of infection he has is setting in is bad. The thing about having an IQ of one hundred and thirty-two is that it's all fun and games to be smart until you feel this level of helplessness. The rest of my cohort has been ordered back to classes, leaving me alone with a perspiring and unconscious Levi. I have been "permitted" by the university to care for him. How kind…

Levi looks like shit, there is no other way to put it. It's boring sitting in this small and uninhabitable kitchen, occasionally running a cold cloth over his head. I decide to stretch my legs to grab something to eat from the other side of the room. Surely it's around lunchtime, but in all honesty, I've lost track of time.

"Hi."

I whip around. Military man. My heart thumps. Why though, I have no clue.

"Hey," I say, standing frozen by the refrigerator. I eye him off as he walks into the room, my eyes locked on him when he stops to stand right next to Levi. He's making me nervous as I watch him fiddling with something in his hands. He looks ... shy? Guilty? I'm getting sick of not knowing what's going on.

"So? How can I help?" I place the sandwich I've grabbed from the fridge down on a plate before taking a small and unsure step towards him. Having an actual conversation with someone who isn't in my close group of friends is like speaking a foreign language I've never studied. Not to mention the fact that he's the first Clean, besides Grenkwist, that I've ever had to talk to for more than two minutes.

He continues rolling the unidentified object over and over in his hands – some kind of canister. Looking over at Levi, he sighs. "I brought these." Holding it out to me, I finally glimpse what he's holding.

"Painkillers," I breathe, relief flooding my veins.

He nods. "I knew he needed them." He looks down at Levi, and I get the chance to inspect him properly. My description so far has been perfect. Military man is pretty; a strong, chiselled jaw, muscular body. This is my first time seeing him out of that damned cream-coloured Lait military uniform. The tight black t-shirt he wears does wonders for him and distracts me from the glaringly obvious.

I'm in danger being alone in the same room as him.

He's a Clean.

I'm a Written.

The realisation snaps me straight out of my stupor, and I rush over to where he stands as he moves closer to Levi. Wedging myself between him and my friend, my heart beats like never before, but I'm not sure if it's because of the danger element or something more sinister … like my goddamn emotions.

"I … I can give them to him." I want to check the contents of the vial first. For all I know, this could all be a cruel trick, and he's hoping to poison us all off one by one.

Military man nods, placing the bottle in my shaking hand. He steps away, an unreadable look on his face.

"Is … is there anything I can do?" he asks, turning back to face me. I know I'm staring, and he appears uncomfortable under my gaze.

My heart slows with the distance he's put between us. My thoughts run a million miles an hour – why does he care? What is he doing here? Why does he keep coming back? Deciding it's the safest thing to do, I shake my head. With no further communication, he simply turns on his heels and heads out to the hall.

"Wait."

I don't know why I say it, or what I'm even going to say next, but he stops. Turning back around, his blue eyes meet mine. "Yes?"

"What's your name?"

His eyes widen, acting like I'd asked if he could use those cuffs that I'd seen him with earlier on me. "Matthew. Matthew Martins."

I nod.

His footsteps head back down the hall as I call out after him, "Thank you ... Matthew Martins."

13

Matthew

"*Thank you, Matthew Martins."*

I hear her voice all day. It's like honey. Smooth and warm, something I've experienced little of as the only son in my family. Niceties were reserved for Arla. Whenever my family addresses me, it's short and stern, as official as if they were speaking to a neighbouring country's representative.

It was foolish, so foolish, to sneak back, but that's what I did the very next day. The one perk of military training is that getting up at two in the morning to creep into the medical centre isn't really that hard. Getting into the medical supplies closet, which is actually locked this time, is harder. Just as I am about to give up, I hear the handle of the room I'm in begin to shake. My head whips around the empty hallway in a frenzy before spotting a cleaning cupboard close by that I can slip into.

I roll my eyes in the dark as I hear an all too familiar voice.

"Thanks for that, ladies."

For once, Flynn being Lait's biggest man-whore works in my favour. I'm furious because he should be in bed and I've let my duties slip, but this feels more important. I'll speak with him tomorrow. Right now, he is the perfect aide as he stumbles down the hall with his arms draped over two women. I bail out of the cupboard and stick my foot out, catching the supply closet door before it closes.

Breathing a sigh of relief, I grab the closest thing that looks like it could help Levi – a couple of bandages. Before I can talk some common sense into myself, I am out the door.

My heart thunders as I stick my head in the room that they have been keeping Levi in.

The kitchen. What a joke. Whether Written are dangerous is irrelevant; the Second Quarter prison has nicer facilities than they have been given. Then I realise Scarlett isn't here. Somebody else is going to find me, and then my life will fall apart, accused of being a traitor.

I hear shifting, and my head whips over to the corner of the room. Thank fuck! Scarlett is here, asleep on an ancient, uncomfortable-looking couch, a tattered blanket held tightly up to her head.

"Scarlett?" I whisper, trying to wake her.

No answer.

"Scarlett." A little louder this time.

Nothing.

I have to approach her. I curse myself, feeling the hairs rise on the back of my neck. Fuck, I'm an idiot. What am I even doing here? A rebel and a red-headed Written that I can't get out of my mind? Is it worth the danger?

I'm standing in front of her now, and she looks so peaceful while she sleeps. Her face doesn't show any signs of worry in the low light. "Scarlett?"

She bursts up from the couch, hands in front of her face, sending me back at least a metre.

"What?! I'm awake..."

Then she recognises me.

"Oh," she says, dropping her hands. It's kind of cute really, that she thought she could fight someone after she was in the most vulnerable and public place to sleep.

And with her thumbs tucked into her fists.

Her breathing slows as she lowers herself back onto the couch.

"What are you doing here, Matthew Martins?"

Fuck. Usually I hate it when people use my full name, but when it rolls off her lips? I shake my head. I will not be entertaining those kinds of thoughts.

All I do is wave, and then inwardly curse my awkwardness. I'm the future leader of the fucking military! I'm not meant to greet people like that! Scarlett looks deadpan, like she is in control of every muscle in her face, not finding this interruption amusing in the slightest.

"Bandages! I brought bandages!" I grab the bag I had shoved them in and pull them out, showing her. My heart pounds as she considers me.

God, I'm so awkward.

"Thank you."

She takes the bandages from me and moves over to where Levi lays. He is at least looking a little better. The painkillers have evidently taken some of the edge off, lowered his temperature and given his body a chance to fight infection.

"He looks better," I say, hoping to get more of a response from Scarlett. She's obviously not a morning person because she only grunts in response.

Pushing Levi's shirt up to reveal the wound on his side, I gasp. I've seen a lot in my time – and yes, I know how old that makes me sound – but this is bad.

I can only watch as she cuts more cloth strips and boils water to clean the wound so she can re-dress it with the bandages that are now lying next to Levi on the table. My nausea threatens to make an appearance, and yet I find myself saying, "Can I help?"

She stops and turns to me. I'm worried I've said something wrong.

"Why? Why are you doing this?"

My heart drops.

"I ... um."

"What? Do you think it's funny or something? To watch the Written girl try to save her friend?"

I shake my head. "No! I think it's disgusting what the guards did to him."

Her eyes widen. She carefully considers her next words before replying, "But he's only a Written."

"He's still human."

14

Scarlett

*H*e's still human.

Not once in my entire existence have I heard a Clean express that notion, the one that we have been trying to prove for over a decade.

Written are humans. We're Lait citizens. We're mothers and fathers and sisters and brothers, just like everyone else. Our treatment is undeserved. My mind keeps mulling it over; surely he didn't mean it? This has to be some kind of trick? I'm convinced he is getting ready to arrest me for the misappropriation of medical equipment. But there is something I truly can't shake. He could be genuine.

He's since brought Levi antibiotics, which I know for a fact are scarce in the Third Quarter, and that's because of the gatekeeping by the Royals. Matthew is clearly taking some risks for Levi. For me. If he is caught bringing the Written resources, well, who knows what will happen. With this information, I don't think twice about what I do next.

I stay up waiting for him the following night.

As I sit here in the dark, I can't help but judge how stupid I am being. Even if he is genuine, it doesn't mean he is coming to see me! I'm probably making his random acts of kindness harder by being here.

Just as I've convinced myself to return to my room – Levi doesn't need as much round-the-clock care thanks to Matthew's medication and bandages – a large frame fills the doorway. *His* large frame.

"Hi."

"Hi."

It's clear that neither of us is any good at *whatever* this is.

Matthew breaks the silence first. "I brought antiseptic." He holds up a glass bottle with sloshing brown liquid inside.

"Thank you," I reply, taking the bottle from his hands. He steps back into the doorway.

"Well, I'll be going."

I look down at the bottle. This contraband is substantial enough that people would get killed for it. And for the Prince's bodyguard to be risking that? All rational thought goes out the window.

"Stay."

Matthew's eyes widen, his face more animated than I have ever seen. "Okay," he whispers, and continues to stand there, unsure where to go.

"Sit." I motion towards the chair next to me.

Keeping his eyes trained on mine, he walks over. "I won't bite," I mutter under my breath as I take in his cautious demeanour.

"What?"

So serious! Biting my tongue, I resist the urge to laugh; instead, a stupid grin fills my face. Matthew visibly relaxes a little when he sees my smile.

"You were joking."

I nod. "No shit."

He lets out a small laugh, and we sit there for a little longer, neither of us knowing what to say.

"What are you studying?"

His sudden question catches me off guard. I'm not used to talking about myself much, and being in this room with a Clean already feels awkward. He's about to discover how uninteresting I am if he's actually here for me and not to play the good guy.

"Um … a mixture of science and research. Basically … um … whatever they tell me."

"What do you mean?" He raises as eyebrow – a perfectly manicured one … Fuck.

I shift in my seat. "Well, Written aren't really given the option of electives."

"Huh?"

"We just do what they tell us to."

Matthew stares at me before falling back into his own thoughts. It's a little while before he speaks up again.

"Is that a normal occurrence? That girl Levi was talking about?" he says, shaking his head as if to rid himself of the thought. "What happened to her was terrible, of course. But what I mean is … do parents leave their children at the border like he said? Or were they just particularly cruel?"

I'm taken aback. After Levi got hurt and I was in charge of helping him, I'd pushed the story of that poor girl out of my mind.

"I wasn't the victim of anything as horrific as that girl, but I was a similar age when my father drove me to the border himself. He didn't blink twice." I feel Matthew's gaze on me, but I keep going, refusing to meet his eyes. "I had a handful of designations at the time. Enough that could have been hidden, with the right clothes and right makeup."

The disbelief coming from Matthew is surprising. Indignance and fury. A look I have only ever seen cross Levi's face when I told him my story as teenagers.

"Why?" he demands.

"My father believed I put my mother at risk. She was prepared to hide my designations, but he thought they were too obvious. She begged and begged him the entire car ride, but he kept driving."

Matthew is silent.

"Then he stopped and opened my door, and like the scared little girl I was, I followed. He stood with me by the border and told me I didn't belong with them anymore."

"What about your mum?"

I shrug, trying not to give in to the emotional turmoil his question brings up. "He'd told her to stay in the car and shut up. She screamed and screamed at him ... until ... um ..." I stop, trying to collect my thoughts. Matthew places a hand on my knee.

"You don't have to tell me."

Shaking my head, I pull my leg away from his reach. "She yelled everything she could think of through the car until my father raised his boot at me and kicked me in the back." Matthew stays muted, waiting for me to continue. "I'd never felt pain like that before. My father worked in construction; he wore steel-capped boots to work every day. That day was no different. From the ground, I looked up at my mother, who had fallen silent. I could see the tears streaming down her face, but that was it. Nothing. She didn't get out to help. I watched them drive away together. We weren't broke, so I've always wondered why they didn't get an erasure machine for me."

Matthew stares off into the distance, his face inscrutable. I wave a hand in front of his eyes, and he snaps out of whatever thoughts he's stuck in. Turning back to look at me with what I can only describe as pity, he reaches out to touch me again.

"Don't," I say, shaking my head. "My father was a bastard, and my mother was terrified. No, that shouldn't have happened to me, but I also won't let it define me. I can't. That girl isn't here anymore, and the best I can do is help other Written in much worse positions than mine. So please ... don't pity me."

Matthew shakes his head. "Pity? No Scarlett. I was going to say how amazing you are. There are few people who could survive something like that and still hold their heads the way you do. You're so strong ... I've never met anyone like you before."

As he heaps on the praise, I start to feel uncomfortable again. There is no way he can actually mean what he is saying, and there has to be some other motive. Noticing that I've clammed up, he raises that perfectly manicured eyebrow at me again.

"I'm sorry, Scarlett. Did I cross a line?"

Did the Crown Prince's bodyguard cross a line when he was telling me how amazing I am? This military man is one hell of an enigma.

I shake my head. "No, it's just ... I'm not used to hearing understanding from someone like you."

"Someone like me?"

"A Clean."

15

Matthew

A *Clean.*

If that isn't a bucket of proverbial ice water, I don't know what is.

I don't know what I was thinking, sitting with her like that. It crossed lines that shouldn't have even been possible. Too close, too personal, too much like I care.

Do I care?

Fuckkkkkk.

Maybe I do.

I'm a dead man.

16

Scarlett

I try not to think too much about it. It's not like we're friends! Sure, we've had a couple of conversations, but Matthew has pulled away after the other night. He's still dropping medical equipment by, but it's always a brief, stiff interaction where he barely even waves a "Hello."

I've spent days ruminating over my last conversation with Matthew, wondering why he hasn't visited again, when I have the horrible realisation that my next demonstration is tomorrow.

Obstacles.

An over-rated fitness test with the occasional bit of problem solving thrown in. I thank my lucky stars that I don't have to study for this one, because between being Levi's nursemaid and this weird thing with Matthew, it has been the last thing on my mind.

Standing from my spot next to Levi, I stretch. My nursing duties have left my muscles cramped. The sound of someone clearing their throat has me turning to face the door.

"Matthew."

There he is, just like every other night this week.

"Hi."

"Hi."

The awkwardness.

Geez.

My turn to break the silence tonight. This would almost be comical if it weren't so forced.

"How are you?" I squeak. What? I swear under my breath as I realise how ridiculous I sound. But why do I care?

"I'm okay. How's Levi?"

Remembering my friend, I break out of my awkward stupor. "A lot better. Thanks."

Matthew waves a dismissive hand. "It's no problem."

"Do you want to talk?"

What ... was I his therapist now? *No!* So, what the *fuck*, Scarlett?

His face is unreadable as he walks over to the couch I've been calling home for the last week. He sits and crosses his legs. There is something oddly endearing about a man with his military uniform impeccably tailored crossing his legs like we are having a gossip session.

I walk over and sit next to him, questioning everything. I've spent my life being told how dangerous the Clean are, and here I am, sitting next to one, unarmed and untrained.

"Can I ask you something?" he says. Meeting his eyes, I nod. "Could you ever forgive someone who helped Lait control the Written?"

Taken aback, I huff and cross my arms, mulling over his question.

Matthew looks away. Almost like he can't – or won't – meet my eyes.

"I suppose it depends on the situation."

A slight tip of his head as he considers my response, but I notice he is still looking away. "If they didn't know better?"

"I think that if they never had the chance to learn I could forgive them, but if they had that chance and still didn't try to understand then I couldn't."

He returns his gaze to me, and I'm struggling not to show how affected I am by his blue eyes.

Not the fucking time, Scarlett.

"My dad kept me in the palace for most of my life. Even when I could leave, it was always on some form of highly orchestrated outing. I never got to speak to people properly. I was always tagging along with the royals, and none of them ever interacted with the Written. I've never even been to the Third Quarter. All this time, I never knew there was a portion of Lait that was so controlled. My focus was solely on myself."

I let his words sink in, and it dawns on me ... Matthew is asking me for forgiveness.

"You didn't know?"

He shakes his head and weaves a hand through his perfect hair. "I should have pushed harder."

"Your dad was in control of you. How are you supposed to know anything when your narrative is so twisted?"

My breath hitches as he considers me. Throwing his hands down, exasperated, he continues, "How? How can you say that? How do you have the control? I'd want to burn the place down. Burn anything or anyone that caused me so much hurt."

I grab his hand, and he stills. "You're delusional if you think that I'm not still angry," I say, shaking my head as his eyes widen. "Not at you," I say, gesturing at our surroundings, "at all of this. How could I have a fair shot at life when others always decide what kind of person I am? You don't get to have a personality or a history as a Written. You're just that – a Written – and nothing else." His eyes hold an intensity I've only ever seen around the Prince. As he goes to speak, I raise a finger to his lips to stop him.

"If I allowed my identity as a Written to control my life, I would have turned down the old woman who discovered me on the border that day. I would have let my reality kill me. I was a child with nothing. Starvation would have taken me. Not to mention my broken back. The Third Quarter is full of so much pain, but it's also full of people that don't judge you for what appears on your skin. Life isn't fair. It never has been ... but there are people that still make it worth trying to find something better."

"You're amazing," Matthew says. I look away, not knowing how to process his compliments. He squeezes my hand, which somehow now sits wrapped in his unapologetically. "You are, Scarlett. I mean it when I say I've never met someone like you."

He's hot in brooding military man mode, but he's even cuter when he's flustered.

"What?" he asks as I try – and fail – to hide my smile.

"I like seeing you nervous."

He breaks out into an uneasy grin. "That's just cruel."

I giggle at the light pink blush that spreads across his cheeks.

"You're like no one I've ever met, either."

Matthew's grin fades into a meek smile as our little back-and-forth dies down. He raises a finger and traces it against my cheek. I glance at him, on the verge of speaking again.

CREAK.

Our eyes widen. Someone is coming downstairs. It seems like both of us have something else to say, but he rushes out of the door and down the hallway without delay. I'm still standing in the entryway to the kitchen when Thad walks in.

"He's okay to be left alone now at night, you can go back to your room."

It takes me a moment to realise he's talking about Levi. Levi. Of course he is.

"Oh, yeah ... I was just making sure."

Thad nods and moves past me into the kitchen. One thought outweighs the others as I return to my room.

Matthew had glanced at my lips.

17

Matthew

I'm relieved to find out the university has postponed the rest of the debates indefinitely – hopefully to cancel them altogether. Tension is still super high, and it seems many of the Clean students have decided Levi is a liar, purposely trying to make them look bad in front of Flynn. After my conversation with Scarlett, I'm more than happy to throw myself into work, and that is why I'm here, following Flynn to the next demonstration.

The only information we received about this next demonstration was the name "Obstacles," so I listen in as Flynn speaks with the Dean on the way to the arena. Well, the Dean had called it an "arena," but as far as I am aware, it's the school's gymnasium.

It's both a blessing and a curse that I'm almost certain Scarlett won't be here.

"...they must dodge and battle tutors, reaching the opposite side of the arena without running into any trouble."

If Flynn nods with any more enthusiasm, I fear his head will fall off. The "obstacles" have him much more interested than any debates. "What do you mean, 'without running into trouble'?"

Gesturing forward as we reach the foyer, the Dean continues, "Students wear a special tracking device that counts the number of touches by the tutors. Once it reaches over twenty, they are considered to be under incident and have failed the exam."

"Why twenty?"

I glance at Flynn. This really is the most interest he's ever shown in anything other than being rambunctious. I can just imagine his father celebrating.

"Since this demonstration is to simulate a life-or-death situation as realistically as possible, without endangering students, we consider twenty hits a sufficient approximation to knock someone unconscious or kill them, depending on the injuries and their severity." I clench my fist as the Dean lets out a humourless laugh. "Besides! Why would anyone want to keep living after twenty possible designations?"

I slow behind them as Flynn agrees, anger flooding through me. I can't believe how nonchalant they are about students potentially becoming Written. Like it's all a big game to them. Scarlett's description of the Third Quarter floats through my mind. Who could ever wish that on someone?

I don't stay mad for long; the Dean opens a door to a private viewing deck, and I'm immediately distracted.

The view that greets us is nothing like the plain-floored gymnasium I'd expected. The space is cavernous, covered in foliage, and I swear I can hear the sounds of an array of animals. It's like the building contains its own little jungle. Flynn and the Dean sit on two plush velvet chairs, the latter looking at me.

"Please ... join us, Mister Martins."

Snapping out of it, I sit down next to Flynn. "Sorry. I'm just amazed. This isn't what I was expecting."

The Dean laughs jovially, glad to see he's still nailing it as an ass-kisser. "It never is. I will have you know that Royal Bennett University is renowned for its arena. The best in the country, if not the world," he gushes. I zone back out as Flynn agrees, like the lapdog he is. The Dean is revelling in all the positive attention. He probably feels like he has to make up for lost time after the debate fiasco.

My mind wanders back to Scarlett. Today is her first day back at classes after Levi was hurt. Not that I've been keeping track, of course. I wonder if she has any demonstrations today. For reasons unbeknownst to me, I'm relieved she's not at risk in this demonstration.

Flynn nudges me, and I look up to see a set of screens slowly rising out of the ground. The Dean smirks at Flynn's reaction, getting a kick out of impressing the Prince.

The screens flicker to life, and my heart sinks.

There are around ten students huddled close together in a small cement room. Five of them are Clean, and five are Written.

Of the five Written ... one is Scarlett.

I try not to focus on her, but my eyes keep drifting back to that red hair as I zone out from the Dean's overview of the rules, until he confidently tells Flynn, "This first round of students unfortunately involves a couple of Written. They are the only ones eligible for this demonstration, but I can assure you the rest of the day will only be upstanding Lait citizens."

Fuck. How have I never noticed the way people talk about them?

Flynn simply nods.

We watch as helpers enter the room and fit the students with what I assume are the tracking devices. These devices look anything but comfortable and remind me of the vests Flynn and I used to wear as kids when we pretended to go into battle. These vests are glowing red. No ... wait ... only the Writtens' glow red.

I turn to the Dean.

"Why are the Writtens' vests glowing?"

My stomach flips as the Dean winks at me before turning his attention back to the students.

This was purposeful. The Written have literal targets on their backs.

Before too long, sirens sound and the rest of the university cohort, who are now all seated on the sidelines, snap to attention. I turn my attention back to the screens and see the chosen students positioned in a circle whilst a tutor speaks. We can't hear what is being said, but the Dean quickly explains that it is a tutor letting the students know the rules.

I recoil in surprise when one screen in front of me splits into nine smaller shots, each showing a different section of the arena.

"Feel free to press the screen when you see something that interests you; that will make the particular feed take up the entire space. Double tap again to see all the views."

My eyes follow Scarlett, and as much as I want to make the screen show her feed in full, I don't. And I won't, at least not until Flynn and the Dean are distracted with something else.

She enters the arena after everyone else in her round. There's no time limit in these demonstrations thankfully, so I ignore the worry about her wasting her time. Scarlett looks around cautiously as she enters. I can't see much from the angle of this feed, so after a quick glance to see that my company is distracted, I swap to one that is a little further away but is easy enough to see her.

I admire her as I watch those clever eyes scan her surroundings, quickly deciding the clearest route. Her file states an IQ that I still can't wrap my head around, and this is the perfect example. Nobody else had assessed their routes. Most have just barged straight ahead. Scarlett moves forward, her eyes glued to the ground.

"Which one are you watching?"

18

Scarlett

I normally avoid the arena as much as possible when I'm on campus. It's too wild, too uncontrolled. Most of the Clean become unreasonable when not under supervision and Written are like shiny toys that they just love to play with.

So, I wasn't overjoyed when I saw where the obstacle demonstrations were being held.

As soon as they switch the tracking vests on, I know this will not be easy.

I always think the Clean can't get worse, only to be proven wrong.

I stay behind the pack that rushes through the door, noting which way they go. The rules are simple ... twenty hits and you fail, and I don't think it's too much of a stretch of the imagination to believe that the tutors won't be the only ones to target students. Student on student fighting is virtually inevitable.

I'm met with three paths once I finally get to see through the doorway.

Along one path, the grass is trampled severely. Most of the others had gone that way. The second is less used, but I quickly note the handful of broken branches. I'd seen a couple of people go that way, but the sheer amount of destruction shows more, meaning some of the less stealthy tutors are clearly in that direction. The third path appears as if it hasn't been used at all – a collection of rocks leading towards a path under an overhanging rock face.

Well, path number three it is.

Taking my time and trying my hardest not to leave too many tracks behind me, I balance precariously on the stones and make my way to the vines that hang over the path.

I'm on high alert, every small sound making me whip my head around. I feel justified in my route of choice as I realise the path is rising from the ground, leaving only myself and a rock face to worry about. There's no way a tutor could hide themselves here.

19

Matthew

I've never been so grateful for my father's training as I am when my fingers flick over the channels ... quick enough that Flynn doesn't have time to see who I was looking at.

Shrugging, I play it off in case he noticed how quickly I switched screens. "Some dude just got cornered by two tutors. He's already at ten hits."

Flynn's eyes widen as he looks back down at his own screen. "Which one!"

"Seven."

Thankful that he's turned away from me, I look back at the monitor, which currently shows Scarlett. She still appears to be alone as she makes her way up the side of the arena wall.

The path eventually looks to end at a pile of rope and boulders. Scarlett inspects them straight away, her hands moving swiftly, but I struggle to make out what she's doing.

"Is she weaving a basket?"

My heart thumps at the chance of being caught before I realise Flynn has switched his screen to show Scarlett by chance as well.

The Dean peers over at Flynn's screen. "It appears so. These are one of the many mental challenges within the arena."

"What's a basket going to do though?"

Flynn's question is answered as Scarlett grabs a metal hook just above her head. We watch on in silence as she swings one side of the braided rope across the hook, creating what appears to be a complex pulley system.

My breath hitches as I realise what she's about to do. Scarlett is going to fill one side of the pulley with the boulders and lower herself to the ground.

"Isn't that dangerous?" It would seem Flynn has realised her intentions, too.

The Dean nods, a sly look crossing his face. I watch with my heart in my throat as she slowly tosses one rock after the other into the basket. Slowly, she lowers herself. Flynn and the Dean have already moved on to a different feed, so I feel a little more secure watching her without judgment.

After what feels like hours, she finally touches down on the ground. As the feed shifts, I take stock of Scarlett's surroundings: a blue lake that leaves me wondering how big this place is, and a path going around. This path leads to what appears to be a dense forest – she's walking straight into the unknown.

My heart flutters as I watch her scan her surroundings again. Apparently, I like smart girls.

Then, she does something I never would have predicted.

She dives straight into the water.

I watch as her bright hair disappears under the murky depths and impatiently wait for her to come back up for air. Except she doesn't come back up, and I feel like I'm drowning.

A full minute.

I feel like screaming, begging the Dean to see what has happened, but I remain quiet.

Then a group roams out from the tree line.

"Why are they going back towards the start?" says the Dean, breaking the silence. I'm surprised at how unsure he sounds. Flynn murmurs in agreement while I watch the three Clean students stalk around the lake.

What I see next shocks me. Ripples. The water is rippling, and the Clean students are noticing.

I see the red of Scarlett's hair drawing closer to the surface, and now, instead of wishing she will resurface, my thoughts run rampant with wishes for her to extend her breath, but I know it's impossible. She's almost at the two-minute mark, an amazing feat in itself.

One of the bigger guys, who looks to be the little group's leader, points her out first. Scarlett's eyes widen, and she scrambles for the shore in the opposite direction. The other two men bound into the water after her.

I will her to run faster, but the pair grabs her just as she makes it to the tree line, yanking her back onto the shore of the lake.

"Are they allowed to do that?" I hiss, turning to the Dean. He nods, but at this stage I'm not entirely convinced even he knows.

"Why do you not seem sure?" I demand.

The Dean looks pissed off that I've called him out in front of Flynn, but he keeps a calm demeanour as he cooly replies, "They're not meant to hurt other students, but there's nothing explicit in the rules against it."

Even Flynn frowns. "That's not okay."

"We've never had trouble before."

"Yeah, but isn't this the first time Clean and Written are interacting like this?"

"Yes."

I study the Dean for a moment longer; he's someone I haven't yet worked out, and he looks bothered at how uneasy Flynn is about the issue unfolding in front of us. Perhaps he assumed Flynn would be okay with watching another brutal beating of a Written?

"They're fucking waterboarding her!" Flynn exclaims, and I don't want to look. I know I can't watch this.

20

Scarlett

Spotty clouds appear in my vision as I plead with the men above me to let me go. They've pushed me under three times now, and each time they pull me back out and dunk me back under, I fear I'll lose consciousness.

"I don't understand," I gasp, sucking in the tiniest bit of air I can manage. "Why are you doing this?"

The biggest one just grunts with a sick smile on his face. "You're that little bitch that hangs around with the guy from the debates."

"Yeah."

"Slut."

The next time they bring me back out of the water, I almost breathe a sigh of relief as they take turns pummelling me in the stomach instead.

"So, what's it like to be a filthy Written?"

I resist the urge to roll my eyes before answering, "Oh, you know ... *oooft* ... lots of witchcraft and mind ... *grunt* ... fucking."

The big one gestures at the other two to stop and takes a step closer to me as the other two hold me up. I school my face and attempt not to flinch as his rough hand wrenches my chin up to look at him.

"You don't deserve to be here, and neither do any of your friends. I wish the Bennett family would hurry up and approve Written culls." He drops my chin. "It's a shame, though. I'd definitely fuck you if you weren't so fucking disgusting." My skin crawls as his eyes rake over my sodden and battered body.

I know I shouldn't, but I can't help myself. Gritting my teeth, I chide, "Oh yeah? With the tiny dick you're clearly trying to hide?"

His friends snicker, and the big guy's eyes flash. It's at this moment that I know I've said too much.

21

Matthew

I'm going to throw up. Right now. In front of my best friend and the Dean of Lait's most prestigious university. I don't know how I've gotten so attached to someone I wasn't even supposed to meet, but I know I can't watch her get hurt like this without intervening.

"Surely someone will stop this?" Flynn asks as we watch the Clean students punch her in the stomach.

The Dean shakes his head. "Not until her hit count reaches twenty. Then, tutors are notified of their locations."

With my eyes wide, I resist the urge to point out how insane that is. "But she's taking actual, proper hits."

I tune out from the Dean's undoubtedly weak reply as I notice they have finally stopped hitting her. The biggest one speaks to her, his hand under her chin. My skin crawls at the action – how dare he!

But then I stop, aware of my thoughts.

Why do you care, Matthew?

The only thing I know for certain in this moment is that I want to sever the slimy hand that touches her like that. My heart pounds as the larger guy steps back. He takes her from his friends, her body weak from the water and the onslaught of punches. His stupid friends watch as he drags her by her hair, further into the deepening water. Scarlett claws at him, but it's no use. Utterly helpless, I stare in disbelief as the Clean student approaches the rocks on the other side of the water. He's going to kill her.

"No!"

Flynn and the Dean look at me like I have three heads, varying degrees of surprise animating their features. Although I know speaking out loud will mean I have a lot of questions to answer, I don't care anymore. I feel sick watching on as the Clean student pounds Scarlett's head against the stone. No one could survive that.

Flynn is the first to notice the group of tutors running through the tree line. My heart soars. They might be able to help her? But at what cost? If they know where she is, then she's definitely taken twenty hits.

As soon as the big guy and his cronies see the tutors, they stop, Scarlett's body sinking back into the depths by the rocks. Two tutors corral them away from Scarlett, and the third wades into the water to retrieve her.

I sit catatonically, watching as they resuscitate her. I won't take another breath until she does.

"Is she dead?" Flynn squints at the screen, looking pale. I don't think he's ever witnessed death before.

After what seems like an eon, the tutors roll Scarlett onto her side, a torrent of the filthy water pouring from her mouth. Relief floods through me.

She's still alive.

Thank god.

It's around four in the afternoon when Flynn and I make it back to his quarters. I ignore him as I make my way past, dead-set on showering the day away.

I've barely made my way into the bathroom, my shirt already in my hands, when Flynn sticks his foot in the doorway, stopping the door from closing. He enters, closing the door behind him, watching me as I make my way over to the shower.

"So, what was that all about?"

"What was what all about?"

"With the Written girl in the first group?"

I turn away from him, grabbing the knob of the shower and aggressively yanking at it. "I just didn't want to see someone die."

"That's bullshit, Matthew, and you and I both know it."

He only ever uses my actual name when he is super serious ... and Flynn never likes to be serious.

He moves closer to me. "So? What is it?"

Although for the past couple of years I have been learning to treat Flynn professionally and less like my best friend, I still struggle to lie to him.

"I ... We ... I know her." I can't look him in the eye.

Flynn can be a lot of things – rash, unreasonable, like an adult toddler sometimes – but I could always count on him not to jump to wild conclusions. If I had told anyone else what I just admitted, they probably would have charged me with treason immediately.

"How?"

That was murky. I couldn't tell him I'd been finding excuses to visit her every night. "The Dean asked me to bring the Written medical supplies."

Flynn raises an eyebrow. "Medical supplies?"

I notice he is now tapping his foot. "So, from one conversation ... you're friends now?"

"It was a couple of times."

Flynn rubs his temples. "What are you doing, man? They're dangerous! And liars! Now you're acting like ... like ... *fuuuuuck.*" Breathing deeply, he runs a hand through his hair. "You like her."

That wasn't a question. I don't move. I can't. I'm frozen to the spot, Flynn's eyes boring into mine, reading all of my darkest secrets.

"You do!" He paces around the small bathroom. "That's fucked! Has it been so long since you've been with a woman that you're resorting to this now? Do you know how much risk you are at by being in the same room as her? That you're putting me at risk? Do you even care!?"

He's right. The King loves his son, but he won't stand for any kind of treason.

"I don't like her like that! It's just been interesting to talk to her!"

Flynn's eyebrows are knitted so dramatically across his forehead that on any other day I would have pointed out how stupid he looks ... I know he doesn't believe me, and to be honest, I'm starting not to believe myself either.

"Just don't get caught, okay?" he says, turning on his heel and leaving abruptly, the door slamming shut.

Flynn Bennett, the Crown Prince of Lait, a staunch supporter of the Written reforms, a playboy ... but when it comes down to it? He is still my best friend.

He may not understand why I'm friends with Scarlett. Hell! I don't know why I'm friends with her, why she seems to rule my every waking thought. But all things considered, he has my back.

Or so I hope.

I triple-check that Flynn is asleep.

There's no noise coming from his room, so I feel confident about slipping out the door unnoticed. Into the night I stumble, my military uniform collar hitched right up to avoid the cool bite of the wind. Heading towards the medical building has become like second nature from the days when I was taking supplies for Levi, so the trek is easy. However, what's not as easy is working out which room Scarlett is in. I thank my lucky stars that it's nighttime and the university only has a minimal amount of staff working, making it easier for me to glide unnoticed past each window.

Making it past most of the single rooms, my heart drops at the sign ahead.

Critical Condition.

God, I hope she's not in there.

The critical condition ward is one big room, allowing nurses to have quick access to all the patients. My eyes scan each bed, my heart lifting a little as I can't see her in there.

But then I see the shock of red hair I've been dreading, in the bed furthest away from the door.

Scarlett looks so small, so vulnerable. My heart breaks as I take in what they have done to her. Before I can make my way further into the room, I hear voices approaching from behind. My eyes dart to any escape route, and I take the hallway that leads off to my left, walking calmly so as not to raise any suspicions. I stop at a water fountain when I realise who it is. Levi.

"She's still unconscious?" he says.

The nurse that's with him hums. "Yes. She'll be okay. She needs time for her body to wake up."

"This is bullshit!" I flinch as what I assume is Levi's fist smashes into a wall. "I can't believe it! If I see those fuckers, they're dead."

"Levi, you and I both know that will not help anything. You need to be here for your friend. That is all … just like she was there for you."

Their voices fade as they enter the room.

I can't help but let my mind wander away from Scarlett and to why the nurse sounds comfortable with Levi. Is she a Written? Do they even have Written nurses?

22

Levi

Fury floods through me. I've never wanted to hurt someone as much as when I saw them bring Scarlett into the Critical Condition ward. They could hurt me all they want, but hurt her? That was crossing a line. Scarlett has done nothing but keep her head down and study. We expected challenges at Royal Bennett University; we knew it would be hard. Hell, it is practically impossible. None of the students want us here, and the faculty staff only put up with teaching us because their wages increased.

Betraying myself, I grab Scarlett's hand. It's early afternoon, and she's stabilised now. I'm just grateful that for whatever reason, she's getting better treatment than I did after the debate.

"I'm sorry," I whisper, her battered and bruised face looking more ominous in the dark-lit ward.

Beep.

Beep.

Beep.

Low, monotonous, irritating ... I want to throw the machine through the window, but it's the only thing that the nurses are listening for so they know that she's alive.

"This is my fault."

I've already filled in the blanks, and I know that if the tables were turned, she would sit and tell me I had nothing to do with it, that they were just pricks. She'd never face the truth – that they targeted her because of what I said at the debates – although everything I said was true.

It's a lot later that night when I make my way back to Scarlett's bed, alongside Sabrina, who I met not long after starting at Royal Bennett. She'd offered for me to shadow her during my spare time. And I'd figured that any knowledge I could pick up in the medical unit here, I'd apply back in the Third Quarter.

As we turn the corner, I notice a figure standing by the window. One that hurries down the hallway as soon as it spots us. I'm sure

Sabrina hasn't noticed, but I have.

Military uniform.

One of the guards that I've seen with the Prince. The one that was bringing medical supplies – the one Scarlett assured me was safe. Was this his doing? Did he put those Clean students onto her?

I wince as I slam my fist into the wall, a massive overreaction to whatever Sabrina has been saying, but I'm furious. Scarlett has spent most of our adult lives trying to help me with my anger, but I just can't shake it.

The Clean are going to kill us.

I refuse to let that happen.

23

Scarlett

"**M**atthew?"

I jerk out of sleep as a hand rests softly on my shoulder.

"It's me."

Levi.

FUCK!

"Oh, of course," I mutter as I rub my eyes clear, hoping he'll ignore my faux pas.

I pull myself up from lying down, wincing as the jarring movements give me a headache. Levi's face is blank, and for a guy who wears his emotions on his sleeve? That's scary.

"How are you feeling?" he says, eyeing me cautiously.

My stomach is uneasy. He's acting *really* weird.

"Like I got hit by a car, then a bus, followed by a plane."

A smirk spreads across his lips before he returns to his neutral expression. "Well, you essentially did. Pretty badly."

I nod but quickly stop as the room spins. Slamming my eyes shut, I will the feeling to go away. "How long was I out?" I murmur, palms pushed against my eyelids. Everything hurts.

"Twelve hours."

"Fuck."

The uneasy silence that falls between us is deafening. Usually, he would crack a joke, or I would nervously chatter about something random to distract him from my hopeless crush.

But right now ... nothing.

I peel my eyes open again and let them rake over him. He looks exhausted, but also as though every atom in his body is on high alert. He shifts ever so slightly where he sits, like he can't quite get comfortable. Despite Levi's dislike of being on campus, he always seems to calm down when he's around me, so I'm surprised there's no sign of that today.

"Levi? What's wrong?"

He raises an eyebrow and keeps his voice measured. "Nothing. Why would anything be wrong? I'm only looking at my best friend, who had her head bashed in by some filthy Clean."

I groan. "Don't bullshit me, Levi. I'm not on enough painkillers to deal with you and your sarcasm."

His jaw ticks, and I know I've hit a nerve.

"Come on, you can tell me anything."

He springs up, the chair scraping aggressively across the tiles. "How long have you been fucking around with a Clean?"

So he has finally lost the plot.

I look around to make sure the other patients aren't paying too much attention. "What?" I whisper as quietly as I can. "I haven't! I don't have a death wish!"

Levi stares at me, silent. "What about the guy who was bringing medical stuff?"

"Who ... Matthew?"

I instantly realise my mistake.

Levi is beyond furious. He's a man who always speaks his mind, shouting for the world to hear when upset. But right now? He stares at me. And I can't bear his scrutiny. I reach out a hand. "We were talking. I was being nice. He was putting a lot on the line to help you."

"Are you *kidding* me, Scarlett? HE was putting a lot on the line? HE DOESN'T KNOW THE FUCKING MEANING!"

"HE SAVED YOUR LIFE!"

"WELL HE SHOULD HAVE LET ME DIE!"

Finally, a couple of nurses who must have heard the commotion come running into the room, distracting us.

"Is there a problem here?"

Levi holds my gaze.

"Levi was just leaving."

Anger is an emotion I am well acquainted with when it comes to Levi – he runs hot-headed. Betrayal though? That expression is unusual for him, and it's plain to see on his face as he nods, following one nurse out of the room, while the other comes to take a set of obs on me.

Growing up together in the Third Quarter, we've had a lot of arguments, but there's something in the air that makes me feel like this has crossed a line.

And I can't deny one thing. The butterflies that I normally feel around him?

Gone.

I'm finally moved to a private room, deemed safe enough to be on my own. It's small and cozy, and far more advanced than any public building we have in the Third Quarter. The bed has a remote control that I've spent the last hour playing with, marvelling at the things in the room that it can do. I rejoice when I find the button that opens the window, and my room is flooded with the cool night air as I turn off the overhead lights. Stargazing isn't a luxury I've been able to do much, so it's nice to pause and admire something so low stakes.

"It's beautiful, isn't it?"

I don't need to look away from the window to know his voice. I've been replaying it in my mind since our last conversation. His steps echo on the tiles as he approaches the bed. I imagine how Levi would lose his shit about me having my back turned to a Clean, let alone one with so much training, but right now? I can't bring myself to care.

"Yeah ... it is." I take the moment to steal a glance at him. He is already staring at me, and my hands sweat under his gaze, my lips tingling, wondering what it would feel like to kiss him.

"What?" I murmur nervously, so grateful that Clean can't read minds.

Matthew smiles. "You look so much better than you did earlier."

He'd been to visit me earlier? I laugh it off, muttering something about looking like shit as he sits on the lone chair, meant for the visitors I will not get.

"Why do you do that?" he says, crossing his legs.

"Do what?"

"Talk down about yourself."

Invisible Levi is screaming in my brain about finding out what his actual motive is, but as I look into his eyes, Levi is forgotten.

"The world talks down to me. I guess sometimes I beat them to it."

Matthew stands and walks over to me. I look up at him, all blue eyes and strong muscles, the epitome of danger. He's a walking weapon, honed to do exactly what the royals want, but his facial expressions? His actions the past week? They seem nothing but genuine. Levi might never fathom that there might be a Clean on our side, but I can't let the idea go.

"Fuck the world."

My cheeks flush under the intensity of his gaze. Against my better judgment, I grab his hand. Matthew's eyebrows shoot up, looking as surprised as I feel, but he doesn't pull away, his hand moulding perfectly with mine.

"Thank you."

"For what?" he mutters, his voice gravelly.

"For making me feel like I'm something more than the designations on my skin."

He squeezes my hand, and I notice as his eyes flick to my lips … again. I return the pressure, warmth flooding every cell where our hands meet, my heart fluttering, breath caught. Am I going to let him kiss me? Is that what this is? Does he actually think...

"Matthew?"

The moment is instantly broken. He drops my hand as we both awkwardly look toward the door. My hand feels empty, cold without his.

Apparently, I've lost all common sense.

"Sabrina. I was just asking Miss Weatherwood some questions. Especially after what happened."

The nurse nods and backs out of the room, muttering something about "letting him get back to it." Matthew turns back to me, his official façade gone.

I berate myself. How could I have been so careless as to grab his hand? There's no future here, if that's what he even wants. It's so utterly impossible.

"Scarlett?" Matthew grabs my hand again before continuing. "Can I ask you something?"

I can't speak. So I nod like a downtrodden child, wondering where all of this is going.

"I'd like to get to know you."

Shifting in my seat, I shoot him a smile. "That wasn't a question, Matthew."

"I'm getting there," he retorts, a small smile gracing his serious face.

"Would you have allowed me to kiss you if the nurse hadn't interrupted?"

Words have eluded me at this point. My body moves before my consciousness catches up, nodding.

Matthew smiles, a light blush colouring his gorgeous cheekbones.

"That's, um..." We both laugh softly, acting like twelve-year-olds with their first crush.

"Kiss me now?"

Matthew's eyes widen, and I'm happy that I finally caught him off guard.

"Are you sure?"

"Please."

24

Scarlett

e kissed.

Fuck.

I wanted him to kiss me, and it was fucking great, but today all I can think about is what this means. We'd been careless, stupid. Whatever this is? It can't go on. Not without landing Matthew in jail, and more than likely sending me to a public execution.

But I want to kiss him again.

Hell, I want to climb him like a tree – not that my injuries will let me.

I want to talk to him openly, not in secret in the middle of the night. I want to meet his mother, who he'd mentioned before he left as the only person who saw him for him. My knuckles ache to punch his father in the face.

Am I too far gone?

Probably.

I'm able to return to the Written dorms later today. Thad had muttered something about shitty treatment as he picked me up, but I don't care. I knew from the outset that they were only going to do the bare minimum. Hell, the only reason I was there at all was because the university couldn't deny that I was the victim.

The one nurse who had been kind to me, Sabrina, told me to stay off my feet for as long as I could. That wasn't much of a problem. My last scheduled demonstration, Special Skills, would see me back in the labs, and I still have a couple of days before then.

I almost cry when it becomes obvious I have to walk back to the dorms.

As Thaddeus helps me around the corner to the pathway that leads to the Written building, I stop. He releases me straight away, afraid that he is hurting me.

I shake my head. "No, it's not that."

Fuck, I'm winded from walking. Those pricks have done a number on me.

As I lean against the side of the building, Thad looks me up and down, concerned. "What's going on? I know the nurse said you need to rest, but..."

I shake my head, cutting him off and resisting the urge to tell him I'm fine. Instead, I have other information that I'm desperate for. "What happened to Levi?"

Thad's emotional openness presents a double-edged sword. It's easy to get an answer out of him, but he also doesn't sugarcoat things. I see his face fall straight away. Even though Levi left in a huff, and we were both angry, I missed my friend.

"He's ... um? He didn't take your injuries well." I stare at him, gesturing for him to continue.

"He went back home and told the university to get fucked."

"What the fuck, Thad?"

Thad raises his hands in mock surrender. "Scarlett, I tried to stop him. So did everyone else, but the uni let him leave."

They let him leave? After dragging us here in the first place? I don't know what to think.

"Have you heard from him since?"

Thad moves over to me and sweeps his arm under my shoulders, propelling me to walk again. I crane my neck as far as I can. "Answer the question, Thad," I huff as we continue to move along.

"No. We haven't."

But there's something in his tone that makes him hard to believe.

My heart sinks when Matthew doesn't visit. He hasn't been for three days now, and even though I know this ... whatever *this* is ... can't turn into anything, my delusional hopes are dashed. I sit on the bed in my room, looking out the window and enjoying my last chance at admiring the skyline, the night before the Special Skills demonstration. Written are getting sent home for the semester break after we complete everything. I've tried, and failed, all day not to think of Matthew and to seek a glimpse of him in the crowds. But I can't see him anywhere. My mind also can't help but wander to Levi. I still haven't heard from him, and I can only hope that our roommates have been talking him down from his anger.

"Fuck!" I yelp, as Matthew's smiling face fills the window frame. "You scared me!"

I let him in, holding a finger to my lips to let him know to be quiet. He clambers through the window, falling onto the opposite side of my bed. I stifle a giggle, but it doesn't work.

"That was graceful," I whisper, my heart thundering at the sheer sight of him. He grins at me, chest heaving and with a bead of sweat lining his brow. "Did you seriously just climb two stories?"

He nods. "Yep."

Am I blushing? It feels like it.

"You know, most girls will get worried if someone kisses them and then doesn't talk to them for three days." As soon as it's out of my mouth, I curse myself – needy much?

Matthew's eyes meet mine. Damn him and his beautiful blue eyes.

He crawls forward, forcing me to lie backwards on the pile of pillows I had at the top of my bed. His legs thread between mine as he holds himself over the top of me. Every instinct, everything I've ever known about the Clean, goes out the window. Right now? All I want is for him to kiss me again.

He reaches up, brushing a stray hair out of my face. A sigh escapes me as his hand trails along my jaw. His face inches from mine, he whispers, "Can I kiss you again? Please?"

Why does this man render me speechless? I nod, and I've barely finished moving my head when his mouth slots over mine like no time has passed, like we do this all the time. Taking his kiss deeper, I wrap my arms around his shoulders, forcing him to put more of his body weight on me, and fuck, I love it.

Common sense? I don't know her.

Matthew pulls away first, a pained look across his face as he sits back down on the opposite side of my bed, creating as much distance as possible between us. He stares at me with an intensity that can only be described as ravenous, his gaze burning a path across my body. It's the quickest of actions, but I don't miss it. His eyes flick to my legs, and it is in that moment I realise what I am wearing.

Shorts.

The designations scrawled on my legs are clear as day.

My face flushes, and I shift my legs awkwardly, hoisting myself up off the bed so I can tuck them under my body. Matthew grabs my ankle with lightning-quick reflexes. For someone so highly trained, he is surprisingly gentle. He rubs a small circle with his thumb.

"Don't. Don't hide from me."

Fuuuuuck. His thumb continues to move as he meets my eyes again.

"I want to kiss you again."

"Why don't you?"

He leans back, his hand leaving my ankle, and sighs. "Because that's not what I came here to do."

Oh. Not sure where this is heading, I lean closer to him, this time pulling my legs under me so I can rest my chin on my knee, and Matthew doesn't stop me.

"My father has sent word that he wants me to step into his role. Effective in two weeks. My father was diagnosed with a mysterious illness a couple of months ago. He's refused to show any weakness for as long as I've been alive, so he sure as hell hasn't told me what's wrong. Even my mother hasn't been willing to talk about it. And Flynn can't get the King to tell him what is happening." He leans his head against the wall.

"In a week, there will be a reception at the palace to 'celebrate'. There'll be two people I like at the party: Mum and my older sister, Arla. Oh, and Flynn, I suppose. It's going to be terrible. After I received my father's letter this afternoon, I wanted to call Arla, see what she thought of all this, but it's been so long since I've spoken to my sister, that I couldn't bring myself to pick up the phone–" he pauses before continuing, "Then it hit me. I needed to see the one person who had calmed everything down for me in a long time.

"You, Scarlett. I had to see you."

My heart stops. Did he really just say that? Me? I am speechless and have no clue where he is going with any of this, so I stay quiet as he continues.

"On top of that, my father wants me to find a date. Present her to Lait. Mentioned something about how he presented Mum at his own reception."

My heart drops, and I want to throw up. There it is. The reason we can never be together. He's going to marry a nice Clean girl, just as he should. I look away from him, trying to hide the disappointment that is no doubt obvious on my face. But Matthew has other ideas. He grabs my hand, pulling me toward him ... bringing my full attention back to the present.

"I told him I'm not interested."

Internally, my mind is doing cartwheels ... but sane and rational Scarlett? She's still confused.

"Okay?" I question cautiously, curious where he is going with this.

Matthew smiles, a sheepish grin. "I told him I'd met someone at RBU."

My heart plummets. This man is bad for my health.

"You, Scarlett. I met you."

My mouth moves, but I can't form any words. Matthew watches my reaction with a little snort, giggling at what are most likely the same faces a fish pulls when it's bobbing around in the water.

"Scarlett Weatherwood. Will you be my date to the reception?"

Before my brain can catch up with my heart to talk me out of this, I nod, and Matthew is kissing me again. It feels like a full minute before he breaks off the kiss.

"Thank you."

I bite my lip, staring up at him. "Are you sure you want to do this?"

"More than anything, Scarlett."

Bringing my lips to his, I kiss him deeply. Fuck, I'll never get sick of this.

He stays the night, despite the fact that it's more than dangerous. As much as horny Scarlett wants to take over, we do little more than make out. I lay for hours in his arms, feeling safer than I've felt in a long time. We swap stories and laugh with each other, my head resting on his chest.

We've been sitting in comfortable silence for a while when he declares that he'll pick me up from the Third Quarter himself. I push myself off his chest to look at him. "Are you sure? It's not exactly guard friendly."

"More than anything. If I'm going to lead Lait's military, I want to lead all of Lait, not just the quarters that are 'Clean'. Plus"–his arm skims my side–"I want to escort my date into the reception myself."

"Okay."

"Okay?"

"Yeah."

He swoops down to catch my lips again.

25

Matthew

W arm, safe, home.

Holding Scarlett feels so right, so much so that I can only liken leaving her to the utmost torture, but at around six, that's what I do. I force myself back out the window into the chilly morning air, praying that Flynn is still asleep.

Scarlett is amazing, and the fact that she trusts me enough to go through with what seems like a whirlwind plan makes me like her more. I've already started counting the days until I see her again. My father will call me delusional – and a lot worse – but frankly I don't care. It's time we bridge the divide once and for all. The Written shouldn't be classed as lower-rate citizens because of something they can't help.

I'm so caught up in my thoughts, I don't notice Flynn's bedroom light on as I creep back into the room, and I certainly don't hear him when he enters the small room I've been sleeping in.

"Do you want to tell me something?"

I whip around, eyes wide. "Tell you what?"

Flynn shakes his head, his eyes dark. "Don't fuck with me, Matthew. Where were you?"

"Scarlett has agreed to be my date to the reception next week," I blurt out, knowing full well I cannot lie to him about where I was.

Flynn stares at me, eyes devoid of emotion. "I don't believe you," he growls.

Silence fills the room. I move forward, begging him to see my side of things. "It's not like that, Flynn! She's good! She's safe!"

Flynn raises his fist and punches it through the wall, yelling, "She's a fucking Written, Matthew! You'll be arrested!"

"I won't! I can convince them!"

Flynn takes a step back, shaking his head. "You're actually insane! NO ONE IS GOING TO BELIEVE YOU!"

"I HAVE FEELINGS FOR HER!"

Flynn's jaw drops.

"Or ... I'm starting to have feelings for"–I run a hand through my hair–"I've never felt like this before. Fuck! You don't think I'm not aware of how impossible this is?!" I gesture wildly into the air. "I'm already due to lead an army I don't want to. I'm not looking to make my life harder!"

Flynn stays silent, staring at me with a look I can't comprehend.

"Say something," I murmur, tired of sorting through my feelings and convincing my friend of something I still haven't fully wrapped my head around.

"The man I grew up with wanted nothing more than to fall in love–" I frown, but before I can say anything, he continues, "–and I thought he was mental. Love was something for fairytales, but he still wouldn't let go of the idea of finding his other half. Eventually, I figured it was okay. He wouldn't leave me for someone else, no matter how in love with them he was."

"Fly–"

"Don't." He throws his hands around. "This is fucking insane and will make me lose my best friend. He's standing in front of me, trying to convince me that the world won't implode when he does something unbelievably stupid. This 'love'? These 'feelings'?" he says, drawing air quotes at the term, "Could end up killing us both."

Eyes blurring with overwhelm, I whisper, "Please, Flynn, it won't be like that."

"Don't," he spits, taking another step away from me, his voice rough with emotion. I surprise myself when tears fall freely. He grabs a bag he's packed near the door, one I hadn't noticed when I got back in. He must have known all along where I was.

"I'm going back home, and I hope you take some time to see how fucking insane you're being. I don't want to lose you."

And with that, Flynn turns away from me and slams the door to his room shut behind him, leaving me alone.

26

Scarlett

The Special Skills demonstration goes off without a hitch. This is fortunate, given the other demonstrations' failures. My biggest concern is heading back to the Third Quarter and facing Levi. The university has begrudgingly organised one of its oldest buses to take us back home. It's still better than the truck they shoved us in that first day.

Sooner than I would like, the environment outside the bus window shifts into the all too familiar ruin that is the Third Quarter. Anticipating it, I close my eyes as the bus speeds past the spot my parents had left me all those years ago. I don't want to entertain a barrage of hypothetical scenarios going through my head about what my upbringing could have been like; I'm already nervous enough, with a carousel of conversations featuring Levi playing over and over in my head. I do not know what to expect when I get home, and I can only hope it's not too awkward – with any luck he won't be home and I can get settled first.

Eventually, the bus stops at the market, drawing quite a crowd. We file one by one off the bus as the handful of Clean guards that chose the short straw throw our luggage into the mud.

I walk towards home with Thaddeus next to me, the older man not making any effort for conversation, but that suits me fine. As we round the corner to my street, he waves briefly before continuing on the path. It's cruel that I have to lug my bag home, bruised ribs and all. I huff, shuffling along as I make my way towards our shack. The mud is always bad this time of year, so every step feels ten times harder than normal.

Soon it comes into view.

Home.

Steeling myself, I walk to the front door and pull it open. Except … it doesn't open. Odd. Normally the door is unlocked, as there's normally someone around. I knock loudly, but it takes a full minute before anyone answers.

The door swings open and reveals Zaid in all his six-foot glory.

"Scar!" He pulls me into a hug, my legs swept out from underneath me as I'm lifted into the air.

"Hi Zaid," I say, hugging him back.

Zaid and his boyfriend started dating my friend Mia only a handful of weeks before I left for my first year at Royal Bennett. They'd moved in together not long after at her place down the road. Everything has been such a whirlwind since then, and I haven't realised until now how much I've missed him.

Eventually he puts me down, and I go to move around him so I can get inside, but I'm left frowning when he doesn't move out of the way to let me in.

"Can I come in?" Maybe they're organising a surprise welcome party. It would be just like Tilly to organise something like that.

But something about the way Zaid is acting tells me something more sinister is going on – the shifting of his feet and the furrow of his brow.

"I don't know."

"You don't know? It's my house!"

"I–"

"ZAID! HURRY UP!"

Levi.

My eyes widen. "What's going on, Zaid?"

Zaid looks at me pleadingly. "I'm sorry, Scar."

Then he shuts the door in my face.

What the actual fuck?

My brain can't comprehend what happened as I make my way back along the road I've just walked down, and I keep ruminating on Zaid's expression. Before I know it, I'm standing outside of Mia's home. Well, Mia's old mentor's house. She'd received it after they'd passed away a few years ago.

God, I hope she's home.

After a quick knock on the door, I brace myself for another weird encounter.

Then it opens.

"Scar!"

Before I know what's happening, tears are streaming down my face.

"Mia ... what ... what's going on?"

"Honey." She wraps her arms around me and guides me inside, sitting me on the couch in her living room. My sobs subside, and she offers me a tissue so I can wipe my face.

"It's nice to see you?" she giggles, lightening the mood.

I snort. "I missed you."

"Tell me everything," Mia says, fetching some water and sitting down.

After a lot of crying and confusion on my part, I sit alone on Mia's couch, waiting for her to finish cooking dinner. From what Mia recounted, Levi had come back to the Third Quarter on a warpath, gathering every hot-headed Written he could find. He'd barricaded himself in the house, and she had no clue what they were doing.

During the conversation, I'd asked her about Zaid, and her eyes had filled with tears.

"I don't know what he's doing there," she'd cried. "We begged him not to leave."

It's so unlike him. Zaid is by nature a peaceful person.

"Asher is devastated. I've never seen him like it before. I'm holding it together for him, but then I'm also trying to contact Zaid, and I don't know what to do." Mia cradled her head in her hands while I rubbed her back. "It's okay to be confused. I know how much you care for both of them," I'd said.

Mia had been so concerned that entering their relationship would tear Zaid and Asher apart, although they had assured her they both cared for each other and her very much. I could only imagine what thoughts she was having now. Mia and I had always bonded over a shared ability to overthink.

Mia brings in two heaped-looking plates of spaghetti, and my belly growls. She sits the plates down in front of us and takes another seat.

"Well, now that you're all caught up on what's been going on down here, why don't you fill me in a bit more about uni life ... tell me all about Matthew ... and I expect a graphic retelling of what can only be a gorgeously tanned ass."

"Fuck Mia!" I laugh. "First ... and unfortunately ... I've never seen his tanned ass. Second, I don't know what to say."

Mia's eyes rove over me like she has x-ray vision. I shiver as she looks me up and down; the issue with being friends for years is that she knows when I'm bullshitting.

"You really like him," she whispers, her voice soft and sure. This isn't a question.

I nod.

"You're scared."

"Terrified."

Mia smiles and grabs my hand. "Whilst I can't explicitly say that getting involved with a Clean is going to end well, I know something about taking a risk." I grin. We both know she is talking about kissing her best friend's boyfriend before they were all an item. "Love is fucked and makes no sense."

I pull away. "I don't love him."

"Please. Scarlett … I've known you for years. Don't lie to me. Don't lie to yourself."

Am I lying to her? Thoughts swirl unsaid. Sure, it's great having a high IQ most of the time, but that doesn't mean that my heart stupidly takes over the rational side of my brain sometimes. I miss lab assignments; they are never up for interpretation like feelings are.

Mia leans forward again, despite my pouting like a six-year-old.

"Even if you don't see it yet, I do. Even though I've never met Matthew, if he makes my beautiful, incredible, emotionally closed-off friend happy? Then he must be okay."

"I really want to believe it'll be okay, Mia, and that this isn't some kind of delusional fairytale."

Mia grins and flexes her (invisible) biceps. "I'll take him down if he does anything."

On my fourth day back in the Third Quarter, we finally hear from Zaid. It's early in the night, and I've just arrived back at Mia's house from my run. Since the obstacle demonstration and my recovery, I realised I needed to get on top of my fitness. I'd avoided Thaddeus's street because I knew he'd chastise me for exercising so soon, but I needed something, anything, to get out of my head.

Opening Mia's back door, I slip in and close it carefully behind me. Mia had told me yesterday that Asher hasn't been sleeping well, and I don't want to risk waking him up. It's only as I toss my shoes off that I hear voices coming from the front yard. Tiptoeing through the house, I peek out the front window.

Mia is standing there, supporting the weight of someone slung over her shoulders. *Zaid*! She's speaking to two people I don't recognise. Before I know what I'm doing, I'm out the front door and taking Zaid's other arm around my neck. He groans, barely conscious. Mia's eyes flash at me with worry, likely a reminder that I had broken ribs, but I don't care. He is my friend too and means the world to her. She breathes a little easier as I take some of his weight.

"I swear to god Michael, he needs help!"

The blond male laughs. "He's right, though. You know he is."

Mia shakes her head. "It's irrelevant. He's hurting his friends! Scarlett wasn't even allowed back in her own home!"

It's then that I realise they are talking about Levi. The smaller man, who has been quiet until now, looks at me.

"So, this is the one fucking around with a Clean?" he growls, his voice laced with fury.

My face pales. Is Levi really doing all of this because of Matthew?

"What she does is none of your business. Scarlett is not an idiot. She wouldn't risk our lives for someone who wasn't worth it!"

Is that what I'm doing? Risking their lives? Would I really do something so selfish?

The smaller man snarls at me again. "Whore."

Before I can say anything, Mia slips out from under Zaid, leaving me to hold his entire weight, and has the smaller man gripped around the neck.

"Tell Levi that if he comes anywhere near me, Scarlett, Zaid or Asher again, I'll kill him."

"Yeah?"–he grunts–"Levi doesn't need you. Your little gays and whore are just a blight on his plans. He's got friends in bigger places." He grabs Mia's wrist and pushes her away from him. "Just don't come back begging when he makes everything better around here."

"You're insane." She spits at his feet before turning back towards me and Zaid. Without another word, she grabs his side and begins leading us back towards the house.

We get him inside and lay him down delicately on her couch. She leans down in front of him and presses her palm to his forehead. "He's warm," she hums. "He must have been like this for a while. Infection must be setting in."

I stand back helplessly. Healing isn't an area of my expertise. Sure, I know the basics, but Zaid is in really bad shape. Medical help has always been Levi's specialty.

"Do you have any supplies?" I ask, itching to get out of the room.

Mia shakes her head, her eyes never leaving Zaid. "He needs antibiotics. I don't have any ... Fuck! The Third Quarter itself barely has any!" She pulls up his shirt, revealing a nasty-looking gash on his torso.

"We need to disinfect that wound."

Mia nods. "There's gin in the cupboard."

I race over, grab it, and bring it back over to her. She cups her hand and pours it in.

"I'm sorry, baby."

Zaid's screams wake up Asher. As he rushes into the room, I duck out, giving them some privacy. Asher had helped at the clinic before I left for the university. I believe he has more experience than I do. He would have stayed longer, but as Written injuries and illnesses continue to rise, he was asked to leave because his wheelchair took up too much room – or something stupid like that.

It's hours later when I hear Asher's wheelchair approach my bedroom door, which I'd left open. I'm not in the living room helping, but I sure as hell knew I wouldn't be able to sleep knowing my friends are suffering. He wheels around the corner and smiles at me.

I haven't spoken to him much in the couple of days I've been back, so I haven't noticed how exhausted he looks. His normally sparkling green eyes are dull, and his face is sullen. I make a mental note to check in with Mia and make sure he's eating.

"Zaid?"

Asher smiles sadly. "He's okay for now. Mia cooled him down quite a bit. He should be stable for a while."

"Thank God."

Asher shakes his head, worry drawn across his brow. "He'll still need antibiotics."

I stare at him. How am I supposed to answer that?

"Mia will go to the clinic in the morning and ask," he says.

"Okay."

Asher moves closer to me. "Please tell me you won't do anything stupid?"

"What do you mean?"

He sighs as if I'm a little kid that needs scolding. "I know you, Scarlett, or at least I know that Zaid really cares about you and likes to mention his fiery red-headed friend." I smile, considering the number of times I've told Zaid off for stereotyping me as the fiery redhead, and yet he still keeps doing it.

"Don't confront Levi."

My eyes widen.

Asher continues, "Zaid wouldn't want you to. Mia certainly won't, and I don't either. Something's wrong with him, Scarlett."

My expression must give away my emotion enough because he backs out of the room. "It's late. Get some sleep."

I nod, still wordless as he leaves.

Levi has been my friend for a long time, and I've also been in love with him. I know him. He is all talk. Surely they didn't think it was Levi who hurt Zaid so badly? It must have been one of his overzealous friends. He's spent time with equally volatile companions in the past, but if I know Levi – and I do – he'll be straight through the front door in the morning asking for forgiveness.

I hope I'm right.

27

Matthew

Since Flynn made the call to head home, we're travelling back towards the castle before the Special Skills demonstrations begin. It's bitterly silent between us in the limousine, aside from the road noise and some other traffic, and he refuses to meet my eye.

Never have I been so happy to see the palace grounds as when the guards opened the obnoxiously golden gates. I can't help but think of the poverty Scarlett described in the Third Quarter. Here we are, living like everyone has enough money to survive when even an inch of the gold from that gate could transform the lives of an entire region.

As soon as the car door opens, Flynn jumps out and rushes ahead, ignoring all the typical protocol. I've barely climbed out of the car myself as I see the back of his head disappear into the hall.

The guard who opened the car door raises an eyebrow at me. I shake my head. "The university wasn't everything the Prince had envisioned."

He nods and goes to step back, the typical move that is done in the presence of someone higher ranking.

"Don't Grant." His head shoots up, a frown on his face. "Please take my bags to my room as soon as the Prince has had his delivered."

Grant moves around to the back of the car, instructing the other guards on whose bags go where. Finally, they leave me alone to take in the Palace's grandeur. Home.

Except it doesn't feel like that anymore.

We've only been back a day when I'm summoned to my father's chambers. Assuming it's for the reception, I think nothing more of it and walk coolly along the halls until I come to the large wooden doors that lead into his rooms.

Steeling myself, I knock. His rooms hold no nice memories for me.

A guard swings the door open from the inside and I walk in. I smile as I look at the sitting area my mother has decorated. Little flowers and paintings adorn almost every surface. I want nothing more than to talk to her, but I force my feet towards the door that I know leads to Father's office.

"Come in."

I push through into a cavernous room with books lining every wall. My father and I disagree on a lot of things, but books are not one of them. My heart thunders as I take him in – broad and imposing, standing up behind his desk, watching my every move.

"Hello Father."

"Matthew." He nods, adjusting his tie.

"If this is about the reception–"

"Prince Flynn came to see me earlier."

Fuck.

"He told me about a concerning conversation you two had before leaving Royal Bennett." Father gestures for me to sit on the chair opposite his desk.

I move as if my limbs are made of lead, each step heavier than the last. He's only ever this silent when he's mad.

"Flynn tells me you have claimed a Written girl ... is someone you are in love with.”

“Father–”

“Is that who you intend to bring to the reception?”

My thoughts scramble.

“Answer me,” he yells, voice booming around the space, causing me to flinch. Against my better judgment, I nod.

He stares at me, his eyes wide. I’ve spent most of my life trying to understand my father to no avail, but this is obvious. He is beyond furious.

He takes a step back from the desk, turning away from me, staring out of the single window that occupies the office. Then, he loses his shit.

“ARE YOU FUCKING INSANE?”

“No, sir.” I’ve done this with him before. If I say what he wants to hear, I can probably get out of here without injury.

“What is it then?” He throws up his hands. “Is she a good fuck? Is getting your dick wet really worth risking everything you’ve worked for? Everything I’ve tried to provide for you?”

“No, sir.”

He stares at me.

"She's in your head."

My heart still thunders, but it feels different this time, more like anger than fear.

"She didn't do a damn thing," I mutter.

Before I can look up and see his reaction, I hear the breaking of glass. He's thrown a bottle across the room.

"I'll kill her. Or send my guards to do it. I won't let you throw all of this away because you're under one of their filthy spells!"

My nostrils flare – *filthy spells*. What a crock of shit. "I won't let you."

"What?"

I stand up from the chair. "She's a better person than you and me. Better than Flynn, and certainly better than the King. She deserves the fucking world, and I won't let you take that away from her."

Before I can think, he's making his way around the desk, his hand pressed against my throat, pushing me up against the closed door. I struggle under his pure strength. For someone with a life-threatening illness, he's doing mighty fine.

"Let ... go ... of me," I gasp. Even though I desperately want to claw at his arms and make him release me, I want to show him I'm confident and collected, not scared of him right now.

His eyes briskly search mine, as if he will find answers, his face only the slightest tinge of red. Even when throttling his own son, this man does not break a sweat.

"You're not my son."

Then he lets go, and I fall to the ground, covered in glass from the bottle. I stand up and wipe down my clothes.

My father stands with his back to me.

"It's too late to change the decision. I'll be taking over the military whether you like it, and I'll do it while getting to know Scarlett, and having her next to me."

Then I open the door, slamming it shut.

The moment I leave the office, tears fall as I lean against the closed door, listening to my father trash his office. Am I really going to risk everything for someone I barely know? If this goes south, we're both dead. I'm sure of that now.

I slide to the ground, sobs racking through my body. What am I doing? Why don't I know anymore? My father is a scary man, and I know that, but hearing him disown me as a son is like nothing he's ever said to me before. Not to mention I used her name. Chastising myself, I hope Father forgets it in his anger.

I'm so caught up in the cacophony I hear behind me and my sorrow that I don't notice anyone approaching until a small hand touches my shoulder. Instinctively, I reach out and grab the wrist of whoever it is, pushing them away from my body. Then I realise it's Mother.

"Come with me."

Her brown hair frames her soft features. She shows no signs that I've scared her and gestures towards the door. It's been so long. Too long. Wordlessly, I follow her across the room to the private hallway that leads to her quarters.

If Father's quarters had all the decorating touches of Mother, then Mother's quarters simply upped the game. Everything in her sitting room is soft, just like her, and all the colours are muted, soft and quiet. As a teenager, I mistakenly pointed out that her muted colours were because of Father and the influence he has on pushing down her opinions. She insisted there was power in silence and kindness, and my father strengthened her. With every passing year, I lose the image of the man she described.

"Come sit over here." She leads me to the large couch. She hasn't pointed out that I still cling to her wrist, as if it's my only lifeline. It's only once I sit next to her that she twists her wrist, intertwining her hand with mine.

"I'm so proud of you."

I look up at her, eyes so much like mine, which are fixed to the wall across from us.

"Why?"

"Tell me about your girl."

"Really?"

She nods.

"I don't know how it happened. One day I was there, focusing on my work with Flynn, and the next there was this girl." I stop, but Mother nudges me, encouraging me to keep talking. "She started showing up everywhere. Or I started looking for her – I don't know. Then her friend got hurt, and I brought her medical supplies."

Mother frowns. "Why? Don't the Written students have access to their own?"

I shake my head and recount what Flynn and Scarlett have told me. She's appalled, thankfully. I don't think I can deal with another family member ignoring the needs of Lait citizens.

"Matthew ... I had no idea."

"Neither did I."

Her face is etched with worry. "Seriously, Mother, it's not our fault," I say, grabbing her hand.

She sighs before changing the subject. "Are you sure about her, Matthew?"

I sit back on the couch.

Am I?

"Yeah ... I am."

She studies me intently, a frown still crossing her face, but she no longer looks worried.

"I'm so proud of you," she says again, squeezing my hand tightly.

"Thank you."

Mother shakes her head. "No. Thank you, Matthew. It takes a lot of guts to speak to your father like that. Something I still find difficult. I may have to stand by your father's side, but I will always be your mother, and if you are happy and safe? That's all I could ever want."

28

Flynn

It's only by accident that I hear Dad and Matty's father arguing. I'm supposed to be in my quarters, signing the new contract that will start my post-grad studies at Royal Bennett University, but I'd sneaked out for some fresh air. Ever since we've been home, I can't concentrate.

"Matthew is a smart kid. He'll realise he's being stupid and dump the girl eventually. You have to wait it out."

It's always pleasant to hear my father call Matthew smart, especially when he'd rather die than ever pay me a compliment like that.

"He's fucking lost the plot!"

I cringe. Matty's father has one hell of a temperament; I can only imagine how badly their conversation had gone.

"Give him time. I bet he realises before the reception, and you never have to hear about it again. Return him to training, get his mind off the girl."

As a kid, I'd spent a lot of time wondering why Dad treated Matthew so well. Especially when I'd sit with the nursemaids, holding ice to my shoulder after he'd hit me, or any of his other punishments. As I get older, I've realised it's because he would have preferred Matthew to be next in line, and not me.

I hear Matty's father sigh. "Thank you, Xavier."

Without being in the room, I know my father is patting Matty's dad on the back, like the twisted fucking besties they are. Yes, I don't agree with Matty and the shit going on, but I can still recognise that our fathers together are never a good combination. We had some hope when Matty found out his dad would be retiring soon, but now I'm not sure.

Fuck.

Matthew is going to not only kill himself but doom the rest of Lait to god knows how many more years of our fathers. I have to do something.

It's easy to find the address of the Written from the debates, the one with the temperament; finding the guard's quarters empty is a daily occurrence. Sliding behind the main computer, I'm into their system in minutes, silently thanking the technology course Father had me take last year.

Levi Smith.

There he is, smack bang in the middle of the watch list, at the top of the "lesser" criminals but underneath the murderers and other major crimes. I'd seen the disturbance he'd caused at the debate, and that is exactly what Matthew needs at the reception. Something to remind him that Written will only ever be a nuisance. If he won't accept that they are dangerous, he will at least accept that they aren't worth the hassle.

"Heath?"

The guard who had been following me stumbles.

You'd think they'd realise I know all their tricks. My best friend is the guard captain.

"Your Majesty, I'm so sorry. I wasn't seeking to intrude."

I turn around in my chair and face him. Heath is young, only new to the guard. He's still very much in his "trying to make a good impression" phase. If it had been under any other circumstances, I probably would have hit on him.

"Stop it. I'm glad you're here."

He perks up instantly. It's almost too easy.

"You are?"

The way I have to bite my tongue...

"Yes, Heath, I am. I have a job for you."

Heath practically leaps over to where I sit. "Of course, sir! Anything."

Then I fill him in. Give him the address and hurriedly scrawl down a letter for Levi, detailing the date and time of Matthew's reception. I picture banners and chanting, maybe the occasional flare. Yes, this is exactly what he needs.

29

Levi

I'll win Scarlett back.

She needs to see clearly – I'm doing this to help her. Help us.

Zaid is regrettable collateral damage. We were never good friends anyway, and the others – whatever their names are – guaranteed they'd get him back to Mia safely. Scarlett will be so grateful when I hand her the antibiotics he will need.

The clinic never even noticed when I took them.

I guess that's the upside to the Clean's brutality; the fact the workers at the clinic are always so distracted with helping new patients made it all too easy.

Now I have to wait.

Scarlett will listen. She has to.

30

Scarlett

"ARE YOU FUCKING KIDDING ME?"

Mia shakes her head, the tears too strong to speak through.

"I'm going to kill him."

"No." Mia grabs the front of my shirt. "I won't lose you as well."

I squeeze my arms around her, gripping her tightly. "This is my fault. I won't let you lose any more for me."

Mia pulls back from our hug, levelling me with a look that would shake anyone. "Don't you stand here and pretend to be the saviour, Scarlett Weatherwood. We'll find something else for Zaid."

It's been three days since Mia went to the clinic to find drugs for Zaid, and his condition is only worsening. Someone left an anonymous letter in her mailbox; however, I recognise my best friend's handwriting, and I am not amused.

The fucker has taken the antibiotics.

The three containers that the King begrudgingly gave the Third Quarter, the ENTIRE Third Quarter, are being held hostage by Levi. He isn't dooming Zaid, but also anyone else in the clinic that needs access to our scarce supplies.

"Besides," Mia says, sniffing. "You have a reception to get ready for."

Matthew.

He's becoming the military leader of Lait, and as far as I'm aware, I'm still meant to be his date. But agreeing to that feels like years ago, after everything that has happened since. And I haven't seen or heard from him after leaving Royal Bennett – what if he's changed his mind?

"I don't know Mia."

"I do, though. You not only get the chance to know someone who seems willing to learn about the Clean, but they're also willing to break down the stereotypes. As much as I want to live vicariously through you fucking the hot military man, I also need you to do this for us. For every Written who has been told they don't deserve to live in the First and Second Quarter."

Looking down at my hands, I nod. She's right; Matthew and I have the opportunity to destroy the societal expectations of the Written and Clean.

As long as he doesn't have a change of heart. A week is a long time to reconsider your actions.

Beauty, or at least the idea of it, is something most Written children are taught not to expect. "Now that you have designations, you must hide them" is the Clean motto. So, standing in front of Mia's full-length mirror in a ball gown feels like something out of the most unrealistic book.

"Are you sure Mia's okay with this?"

Asher, who sits in the doorway, scoffs, "Mia's just glad someone can wear it. You'd never guess the number of times I've found her admiring it, sad that she has nowhere to go in it."

Smoothing down the dress, I pivot awkwardly, checking every angle. "This feels so foreign. I don't think I've ever worn a dress before."

"You look great. Stop worrying."

Mia's birth mother had wrapped her in this dress as a baby and left her at the Third Quarter border with nothing more than the red, luxurious silk that was draped over my body right now. It feels uncomfortable wearing something so special to her.

"But–"

Asher raises a finger. "Nope. Don't want to hear it. You look hot, end of story. If Zaid were awake, he'd be making a crack about the colour offsetting your hair. Asher, however..."

I giggle as he refers to himself in the third person.

"He doesn't care about fashion. He doesn't care about dresses, or a happily ever after, like Mia. He cares about his partners and their happiness. Mia loves you; she wants this for you, and so do I."

"Thank you, Asher."

Asher winks. "Please talk to Mia after you sleep with your military man. I don't want to keep hearing about it from her."

My face has to be as red as the dress as Asher rolls away, presumably to the living room where Mia sits with Zaid. I take one last glance in the mirror and frown. My shoes don't suit my outfit. The scrappy high-tops are my bread and butter here at home, flexible for running and walking, and they are all I have.

Facing the prospect of seeing the King and Matthew's family in a hand-me-down dress and faded brown shoes is not ideal, but it's going to have to do.

"Fuck!"

My head snaps up at the noise coming from the living room, where crashing and muffled gasps and groans fill the air.

"No!" Then screaming starts, and I'm out of the room in a millisecond.

Zaid.

I rush into the living room to see both Mia and Asher crowding around a thrashing Zaid, the latter trying his hardest to dab at Zaid's forehead with a cool cloth. Mia stands with wide eyes, her hand clasped to her mouth, tears streaming down her face.

Fuck this.

I'm going to Levi, impending reception be damned. I will not be the reason my friend dies.

The dirt doesn't matter. The dirt doesn't matter. The dirt doesn't matter.

But fuck, it really does! It's impossible to avoid the small blobs that creep up the edges of the dress, and the recent rain has guaranteed every sidewalk is a mudslide. I groan as I realise just how dirty I look, but surely if Matthew is willing to ignore the fact that I am a Written, he won't care about some dirt? Or maybe he will … after all, I don't really know him.

What the hell am I doing?

But there's no point ruminating as I run up to the front door, throwing my weight behind my knock.

"LEVI SMITH! YOU PSYCHOTIC FUCKER!"

I bang on the door, screaming as many profanities as possible until I hear feet shuffling inside. The door swings open, and I stop.

"Levi."

I had expected him to send one of his new friends, so I'm immediately thrown off by seeing him. I step back as he opens the door, closing it behind him.

"Hi Scar."

"Don't 'Hi Scar' me. What the fuck is going on?"

Now that he's outside, I can see him properly, and he doesn't look good. His five o'clock shadow is becoming a beard, and the skin around his eyes is a gross shade of purple. I've never seen him like this before.

"Doing what we talked about."

"You're insane."

"I'm insane? Are you kidding, Scar? You're fucking a Clean! And not just any ... the future leader of Lait's military!"

I brush a hand through my hair. "Are you actually *kidding* me, Levi? If this is all because you're jealous, you are fucking nuts. I'm not 'fucking' anyone! The Levi I know ... *he* wouldn't be holed up here with the only medication that could save Zaid's life! And how many others are you killing?"

Levi rolls his head around, as if to get rid of the tension. "None of what I'm doing is intended to hurt the Written. It's to help! I wish you could see that!"

This man in front of me – he is a complete stranger. Tears brim my eyes.

"This isn't you," I whisper.

Levi huffs, repeating my words back to me.

"This isn't you."

I shake my head. "Don't you dare."

Both of us fall into an awkward silence, each playing an internal war of who will break first.

I hear a car nearby and assume it's the changing of the guard. Some First Quarter assholes who are ecstatic to finish their shift in the Third, I'm sure.

When did his eyes change? I ponder, staring at Levi. I'm used to the shining kindness, but today I find none of it.

Why can't he – ?! I gasp as he closes the small distance between us.

Then ... his lips crash into mine.

31

Matthew

I can't remember the last time I was allowed to drive on my own. That's why I'm even more eager as I turn down the road that leads to Scarlett's home. This feels like a proper date, like maybe we can really do this.

Driving slowly down the road, I keep my eyes peeled on the house numbers.

38! That means the next one is…

You know that moment when the shock is so sudden, it feels like your heart has plummeted from its place in your chest?

That's how I feel as I see Scarlett kissing another man.

Kissing Levi.

Is this all a trick? Is my father correct? Am I just a stupid, naïve boy? Has she played me, just like that redhead who tried to kill Flynn in the bar? Is that Scarlett's endgame? To kill me?

I school my breathing as I watch her walking down the footpath, right towards where I sit. She hasn't noticed it's me in the car yet. She looks furious, which only confuses me further. Surely a rebel wouldn't risk dying like this. I don't know what to think. Before I can decide, I'm rolling down the window.

"Scarlett!"

Her head shoots up in my direction, and she smiles. I've almost forgotten why I was overthinking until she quickly glances over her shoulder. Is she making sure her boyfriend doesn't see me?

Fuck.

I don't know.

Before I ruminate anymore, she's standing at the side door and I'm letting her into the car.

"Hi."

That voice.

God, I want to trust her. I want to kiss her the moment she sits down, but I can't.

"Hey."

My eyes stay peeled on the road as we drive away. I pretend not to notice, but out of the corner of my eye, I see her staring at me. I'm at a loss for words. How are you meant to say, "Hi! I'm so keen for our first date, one that might destroy our society, but also … um … why were you kissing your best friend a moment ago?"

Exactly.

My brain runs through countless theories, and I covertly scan her for any signs of lying.

I'm not a man of many words at the best of times, let alone when all I can feel is my heart cracking at the edges. Have I imploded my life for a girl I barely know?

32

Scarlett

Is he having second thoughts?

I fidget with my hands for the entire car ride.

I've tried my hardest to talk to him, but he's barely giving one-word answers. Maybe he's nervous? He is about to become the head of the military after all. That has to be it! He's nervous.

It's not me.

Hopefully.

I rub my mouth, desperate to get rid of the feeling of Levi's lips on mine. It amazes me that over a month ago, I would have been giddy that he kissed me, and now I want to sanitise my face.

My jaw drops to the floor as we pull up to the gates of the palace.

Gold gates!?

The palace is only ever somewhere I've seen in pictures, and pictures do not depict just how grandiose it is. I squint at the building, almost certain that the windows are lined in gold as well.

"This is insane," I whisper.

Matthew grunts. "The porcelain prison."

My heart drops. This is his home, the place where he grew up. And from what he has told me, it's a place he does not want to be.

"I'm sorry."

Matthew turns his head to me as he drives through the now-open gates, the first hint of a smile on his face. "Don't be. I had everything I ever wanted."

"Except freedom."

For a split second, I catch his guard down, and with a small, genuine nod, he replies.

"Yeah."

I expected looks.

But when every single person leaves at least a metre of space around me? It gets overwhelming – fast.

All of Lait's high society is here, and nearly all of them are staring straight at me. We've barely made it into the building as I hold on to Matthew's arm for dear life.

"Can we talk?"

His voice is so soft in my ear, it takes me a moment to register he is talking to me.

"Oh ... yeah! Of course? Except, are you allowed to leave?"

Matthew scoffs, "It's my party."

"Okay." I squeeze his arm. "Lead the way."

It feels like one opulent hallway after another until he pulls me into a room. I assess my surroundings; I'd expected a lot of things in the palace, but an art studio is not one of them.

Every nook and cranny is filled with completed and half-finished paintings. The floor is splattered in colours, like the artist has no care for how meticulous the rest of the castle is. I stop at a canvas that has been propped up in the middle of the room.

Reds and yellows make up a stunning, but violent-looking rose.

"Is this real to you?"

Matthew.

I look up and see him standing against the closed door, his eyes searching me like I've only ever seen him do around the Prince. This isn't Matthew I'm talking to. It's Lait's newest military leader.

"What do you mean?"

"I saw you."

"You saw me what?"

Matthew sighs. "I saw you kiss Levi."

I'm going to throw up. That's why he's acting weird? Did he not see when I pushed Levi away? Or when I punched him?

"He kissed me," I say, crossing my arms defiantly.

Matthew shakes his head. "That doesn't make it better. Are you with him? Why are you here? I won't let you hurt the Bennetts."

My heart drops. Anger courses through my veins. I am so far out of my comfort zone here, it is unbelievable to me he can think I will do anything to jeopardise this … us.

"Maybe if you'd paid more attention, you would have seen me push him away."

Matthew's eyes widen. And despite my best efforts, tears run down my cheeks.

"If you weren't so quick to label me as a fucking Written whore like the rest of them, you would have seen me punch him." I move forward, raising a finger to his chest. "Do you have any idea what I'm putting on the line to be here? If this fucks up for you, you can just blame me for putting some 'witchy' spell on you. If this fucks up for me? I'll be an outcast. Probably dead. Can you even imagine what it's like to be an outcast among the outcasts? I won't survive."

His eyes drift down to my finger, and he grabs my hand. Against my better judgement, I let him.

"Scarlett, I'm sorry. We obviously don't know each other well yet, and my jealousy mixed with my fear turned me into something I don't want to be anymore. Can you forgive me?"

This complicated, beautiful enigma.

"Of course. I probably would have jumped to the same conclusion if it were the other way around. Just ask me next time," I huff.

"Okay."

"*Okay ...?*"

"Can I kiss you?"

"I really wish you would."

33

Matthew

I feel happier than I have in years as I lead Scarlett back into the main room of the reception, both of us disappearing into the crowd. Laughing together, we become caught up in each other, blissfully unaware of our surroundings.

That is … until Father taps my shoulder.

"Son."

I whip around to face him, sensing Scarlett tense beside me, her hand still raised halfway in the air to drink before setting her glass back on the table.

"Hi Father."

"Introduce me to your slut."

I immediately see red.

"Don't talk about her like that," I hiss, gritting my teeth. I'm aware that everyone is watching this interaction unfold between the outgoing military leader and his son.

He places his hand on my shoulder, a friendly movement to anyone watching but a gesture of aggression to me. Especially with how tight his grip is. "I'm sorry, I still outrank you. I'll do what I want."

Blindly, I reach behind me, grabbing for Scarlett's hand and squeezing.

"My life is none of your business."

We stand at an impasse, reminding me of the Western books Arla used to read. I momentarily wonder where she is as my father scolds me with a look that used to work, but I'm reminded of what I have to fight for; Scarlett's hand is a lifeline back to reality.

I turn to walk away when a bomb goes off.

Chaos.

People screaming, running in every direction.

Written?

Rebels.

I'm thrown backwards by a second bomb, this one too close for comfort. Thinking is impossible as my ears ring, my vision blurs and I'm certain that my jaw has taken some serious damage.

Then I see them.

Dressed in rags and face coverings, the rebels are undoubtedly Written. I try my hardest to ID them but can't see through the smoke.

"Matthew, we have to go." A petite hand rests on my shoulder.

Scarlett.

The kiss.

She did this.

She has been working with Levi.

Another bomb explodes, and the blast separates us as we both dive for cover.

I try my hardest not to focus on her and instead make my way through the crowd, getting as close to the rebels as I can. Neutralising them has become my goal. I've never been so happy to be my father's weapon than when I go into soldier mode and forget the betrayal of the woman I care about.

Crawling behind a large piece of debris, I crouch, ready to grab at the closest rebel before I'm distracted by gunfire.

BANG, BANG, BANG!

The shooter steps out from the cluster of rebels. Anyone who is still left in the room stops. A deathly quiet blankets the room.

"LISTEN UP! WE'VE LOST EVERYTHING! IT'S TIME FOR YOU TO DO THE SAME!"

Where have I heard that voice before?

Then, a figure steps out from the other side of the room.

Scarlett.

"Levi, how could you?" she screams.

She didn't know.

She was telling the truth, and I've left her to deal with the bombings on her own. I've left her to die.

Levi stills, pulling his mask down.

"How could I? Are you fucking kidding me, Scar? Do you know how many lives these people have on their hands?"

Scarlett shakes her head, tears streaming down her face.

"Most of these people don't know! They need to be educated!"

Levi throws his mask on the ground. "Educated? They've had

enough time to do that!"

I'm too far away to be of any help during this interaction, but my heart hammers as I make out a guard creeping up behind Scarlett.

"Scarlett, watch out!" I scream, leaping up from my hiding spot and completely blowing my cover. She whips around but is too slow. The guard already has her hands pulled behind her back.

Chaos returns.

34

Scarlett

As soon as Matthew calls out, Levi drops to the ground and the gunfire returns, this time from guards that have rushed into the room. I am helpless as I watch my best friend turn into the monster he never wanted to be. My hands are bound by the heavy hold of the armoured person behind me.

I feel the guard's hold go slack. I wrench my hands free and turn around, watching the man fall to the ground, a bullet through his forehead. Feeling ill, I convince myself that the warm feeling on the back of my neck is not his blood.

I whip around and see Levi staring at me through the crowd, lowering his gun.

"Run," he mouths, before turning back to the throng of guards streaming into the hall.

THE CLEAN

He doesn't need to tell me twice.

I still hear Matthew screaming my name, but I don't dare stop. There are already more guards following me.

35

Flynn

I've never felt pain like this before.

Something that's so consuming, you want nothing more than for it to end.

As time passes, numbness replaces the agony, and the pillar on top of me becomes like a morbid blanket. If I wanted to pretend hard enough, I might even feel its warmth – like a comforting hug that I've never received from my father. But right now, I just feel so deathly cold.

I can do nothing but watch as the guards evacuate my family. My throat is so dry from the dust that I can barely muster a moan, let alone a cry for help. They look like they might be frantically searching for me, but never would they imagine I'm trapped here, under the rubble.

Nobody knows I am still alive. Or maybe they don't care.

If I don't get to the Clean rooms soon, to the machine that can help me, the designations that I know have appeared on my skin will be permanent.

Then I'll be as good as dead anyway.

It is a relief when darkness washes over me.

36

Matthew

As I sit in the back of the evacuation plane, my hands tied together behind me, I can only hope Scarlett has escaped. My father won't answer my questions, and the King sits consoling his wife.

They couldn't find Flynn, so they left without him. I feel like I've failed him. None of this would have happened if I hadn't been so caught up in falling in love. I should have stayed away from the Written, like everyone told me. But my heart still aches for Scarlett, for the need to help and uncover the truth.

I have no idea where we are going. All of this emergency evacuation stuff is above my clearance, something I would have learnt when I assumed my father's position.

That sure as hell isn't happening now.

My mother just stares at her hands, and my heart breaks some more. I've failed her too.

I'm a traitor now.

Continue Matthew and Scarlett's story in **The Break**

Book 2 of The Clean Trilogy

Book 1 – The Clean

Book 2 – The Break

Book 3 – The Written

DISCOVER THEM ALL
www.hopeswan.com.au

Liked this book?

**Please leave a review to recommend
this book to fellow readers.**

Whether on Amazon, Goodreads, an email to the author,
a recommendation to a friend, or all of the above.

Thank you.

The Clean is my first story outside of the Oz series. It's a terrifying thing to take on something new like this, but I'm so excited to show you all the world of Lait.

Thank you to Wattle Tree Press; Brooke, Shelley, and Tara, for being the best publishing team I could have ever wished for and making my first foray out of Oz smooth. This is the first time I've felt "safe" in being able to produce my work, and it's all because of these wonderful women.

Thank you to Ashley Nobes for bringing Matthew and Scarlett to life. (And Flynn!)

There's so much more I have in store for this world, and I can't wait for you guys to read it.

And to those with their own designations, visible or otherwise, I see you. We are the best humans.

Hope Swan is a fantasy author from South Australia. Her first book, Oz, was published in 2024, after her university project turned into something more and she realised her dream of being an author. Hope's books will always have drama, sass, and at least one incredibly sarcastic character that she knows you'll love!

When she's not writing, Hope loves to dance, go to the gym, and put her film degree to good use on movie night!

Find Hope on Instagram @hopeswanauthorofficial or join her Patreon 'Magic, Sarcasm, and Yearning Redheads.

Also by Hope Swan

HOPE SWAN
OZ
ILLUSTRATION BY
MATTHEW BROUGHTON

HOPE SWAN
OZ
ONE WIZARD'S
CARNAGE

HOPE SWAN
ALTHIE
ILLUSTRATION BY
MATTHEW BROUGHTON

HOPE SWAN
THE
GOOD
WITCH

After Dorothy's defeat of the Wicked Witch of the West she went on to become one of Oz's most beloved rulers. *Oz thrived under Dorothy*. Only days before Dorothy is due to announce her predecessor it is announced she is missing. Gone. Without a trace. The Wizard's Coalition takes control of the country within days. Their leader, Marcus Rightfoot elected as the next ruler of Oz. Soon, living in Oz becomes worse then it was under the rule of the Wicked Witch. Delia believes that Oz is a myth. A place that was created to explain the disappearance of a young girl in the sixties. Then a mysterious woman claims she is the Wicked Witch's sister. And that Delia is in Oz. And that Delia is destined to find Dorothy.

Delia has been trying really hard to settle into life in Oz and life as the younger sister of Oz's most beloved ruler. It's a lot of pressure. Then Marcus Rightfoot escapes his prison. Surely that's no big deal! She has Dorothy now and all of Oz behind her. *It'll be fine. After all, how much carnage can one wizard make?*

Althea Westway has been told her entire life that her mutation, her skin, puts her at risk. She's content to stay with her sister and mother, safe in their cottage in the West Country forest. Then one day, after a game of hide and seek with her sister, she meets a young boy. Made of tin. He tells her stories of the world and encourages her to join him at the Marbost school. Nathaniel and Althea are both Ozian outcasts, but know that they can get through anything together. So what goes wrong? ***Althie is a new take on the story of the Wicked Witch of the West and dives deep into the question: Is anyone ever truly just evil?*** *This **Oz** prequel and can be read as a standalone.*

Glinda Michaels has lived in the upper echelons of Ozian society since birth. With parents in the public eye and a twin brother that has the tendency to attract all the wrong attention, she knows how to smile and keep her head straight. Her first year of university arrives and she meets two people that change the direction of her life. The first, a wizard, flirty and confident. The second, the daughter of her father's opposition party in Ozian parliament. Glinda finds herself pulled between her image and her actual desires. Does she toe the line? Or does she risk everything? ***The Good Witch follows everyone's favourite pink loving blonde through her teenage years, her early days in the Ozian public eye and past Dorothy's whirl wind introduction.*** *This **Oz** prequel and can be read as a standalone.*

Wattle Tree Press is an independent publisher located on the picturesque Central Coast of Australia. WTP believes that everyone has a story (or two) within them and aims to bring Aussie storytelling to the wider world.

Their growing catalogue can be found at:

www.wattletreepress.com